William Black

The Beautiful Wretch

Vol. 2

William Black

The Beautiful Wretch
Vol. 2

ISBN/EAN: 9783337417611

Printed in Europe, USA, Canada, Australia, Japan

Cover: Foto ©Andreas Hilbeck / pixelio.de

More available books at **www.hansebooks.com**

THE BEAUTIFUL WRETCH

THE

BEAUTIFUL WRETCH

THE FOUR MACNICOLS

THE PUPIL OF AURELIUS

𝔗𝔥𝔯𝔢𝔢 𝔖𝔱𝔬𝔯𝔦𝔢𝔰, 𝔦𝔫 𝔗𝔥𝔯𝔢𝔢 𝔙𝔬𝔩𝔲𝔪𝔢𝔰

BY

WILLIAM BLACK

AUTHOR OF 'MACLEOD OF DARE,' 'SUNRISE,' ETC.

VOLUME II.

𝔏𝔬𝔫𝔡𝔬𝔫

MACMILLAN AND CO.

1881

Printed by R. & R. CLARK, *Edinburgh.*

CHAPTER XII.

'MANY people have told me I am very like what Nan used to be,' continued Miss Madge, pleasantly. 'And there is a photograph of her——. Let me see, where is it?'

She went to a table and opened an album, his eyes following her with wonder and a vague bewildered delight. For this was a new acquisition to the world—another Nan, a Nan free from all hateful ties, a Nan not engaged to be married. Presently she returned with a card in her hand.

'It was taken at Rome the time Nan went to Italy. That's more than three years now. I think myself it is like me, though it is rather too young for me.'

It was indeed remarkably like this Madge who now stood beside him. But yet sure enough it was Nan—the Nan that he remembered walking about the brilliant hot gardens at Bellagio. Here she was standing at a table, her head bent down, her hand placed on an open book. It was a pretty attitude, but it hid Nan's eyes.

'Yes, it would do capitally as a portrait of you,' he said quickly; 'no wonder I was mistaken. And your sister Edith, has she grown up to be like your eldest sister in the same way?'

'Oh no; Edith never was like the rest of us. Edith is dark, you know.'

Any further discussion of Miss Edith's

appearance was stopped by the entrance of that young lady herself, who was preceded by her mamma. Lady Beresford received Captain King very kindly, and repeated her son's invitation that he should dine with them that evening. And had he seen the Strathernes since his return? And how long did he propose remaining in Brighton? And which hotel was he staying at?

The fact is, Captain King was still a little bewildered. He answered as he best could Lady Beresford's questions, and also replied to some profound remarks of Miss Edith's concerning the rough weather in the Channel; but all the time his eyes were inadvertently straying to the younger girl, who had gone to restore Nan's portrait to its place, and he was astonished to see how this family likeness could extend even to the pose of the figure and the motion of the hand. He could almost have believed now that that was Nan there, only he had been told that the real Nan—no doubt very much altered—was for the time being staying with some friends at Lewes.

In due time he went away to his hotel to dress for dinner—an operation that was somewhat mechanically performed. He was thinking chiefly of what Mr. Tom had told him at the Waterloo Club concerning the young gentleman who had been warned off by the Vice-Chancellor. He had taken little interest in the story then; now he was anxious to recollect it. Certainly Miss Madge did not seem to have suffered much from that separation.

When he returned to Brunswick Terrace he found that the only other guest of the evening had arrived, and was in the drawing-room with the family. From the manner in which this gentleman held himself aloof from Miss Edith, and did not even speak to her or appear to recognise her presence, Frank King concluded that he must be Miss Edith's suitor—no other, indeed, than the person whom Mr. Tom had called Soda-water. Soda-water, if this were he, was a man of about five-and-thirty, of middle height, fresh complexioned and of wiry build, looking more like an M. F. H., in fact, than anything else. His clothes seemed to fit well, but perhaps that was because he had a good figure. In the middle of his spacious shirt front shone a large opal, surrounded with small diamonds.

Captain King had the honour of taking Lady Beresford down to dinner, and he sat between her and Miss Madge. It

soon became apparent that there was
going to be no lack of conversation. John
Roberts, the soda-water manufacturer, was
a man who had a large enjoyment of life,
and liked to let people know it, though
without the least ostentation or pretence
on his part. He took it for granted that
all his neighbours must necessarily be as
keenly interested as himself in the horse
he had ridden that morning to the meet of
the Southdown foxhounds, and in the run
from Henderley Wood through the Buxted
covers to Crowborough village. But then
he was not at all bound up in either foxhounds or harriers. He was as deeply
interested as any one present in the fancy-
dress ball of the next week, and knew all
the most striking costumes that were being
prepared. No matter what it was,—old
oak, the proposed importation of Chinese

servants, port wine, diamonds, black Wedgwood, hunters, furred driving coats, anything, in short, that was sensible, and practical, and English, and conduced to man's solid comfort and welfare in this far too speculative and visionary world,—he talked about all such things with vigour, precision, and delight. The substantial, healthy look of him was something in a room. Joy radiated from him. When you heard him describe how damsons could best be preserved, you could make sure that there was a firm and healthy digestion ; he was not one of the wretched creatures who prolong their depressed existence by means of Angostura bitters, and only wake up to an occasional flicker of life at the instigation of sour champagne.

This talk of the joyous Roberts was chiefly addressed to Lady Beresford, so it gave Frank King plenty of opportunity of making the acquaintance of Nan's youngest sister. And she seemed anxious to be very pleasant and kind to him. She wanted to know all about Kingscourt, and what shooting they had had. She told him how they passed the day at Brighton, and incidentally mentioned that they generally walked on the pier in the morning.

'But you won't be going to-morrow, will you?' he said quickly.

'Why not?' she said.

'I am afraid the weather promises to be wild. The wind is south-west, and freshening. Listen!'

There was a faint, intermittent, monotonous rumble outside, that told of the breaking of the sea on the beach.

'That ground swell generally comes

before a storm,' he said. 'I thought it looked bad as I came along.'

'Why should you prophesy evil?' she said, petulantly.

'Oh, well, let us look at the chances on the other side,' he said, with good-humour. 'The best of Brighton is that there is nothing to catch and hold the clouds : so, with a fresh southerly wind you may have them blown away inland, and then you will have breaks of fine weather. And then the streets dry up quickly in Brighton.'

'But all that means that it's going to be a wet day,' she said, as if he were responsible.

'With breaks, I hope,' he answered, cheerfully. 'And then, you know, living at Brighton, you ought to be half a sailor —you shouldn't mind a shower.'

'Oh, but I do,' she said. 'It's all very

well for Nan to get on her thick boots and
her waterproof and go splashing away
across ploughed fields.   I wonder what
the house would be like if every one went
on in that way, and came home all over
mud.'

However, Madge soon repented of her
petulance, and was quite attentively kind
to the new guest, even reproving him for
not attending to his dinner, and letting
things pass.

Dinner over, Mr. Tom took his mother's
seat, and somewhat grandly sent round the
wine.   As nobody took any, and as starting subjects of interest was not Mr. Tom's
strong point, he suddenly proposed that they
should go into the billiard-room and send
for the girls.   This was acceded to at once.

Now billiards is a game in which a good
deal of favour can be shown, in a more or

less open way. Mr. Tom, having no one
of sufficient skill to match himself against,
chose to mark, and directed the remaining
four to have a double-handed game. Mr.
Roberts immediately declared that Madge
and himself would play Captain King and
Miss Edith. This was assented to in
silence, though Madge did not look well
pleased, and the game began.

Very soon Mr Tom said—

'What's the matter with you, Madge?
Are you playing dark? Have you got
money on?'

Frank King followed Madge, and it
was most extraordinary how she was
always missing by a hairsbreadth, and
leaving balls over pockets.

'What do you mean, Madge?' Mr.
Tom protested. 'Why didn't you put the
white ball in and go into baulk?'

'I don't play Whitechapel,' said Madge, proudly.

Frank King and his partner seemed to be getting on very well; somehow, Madge and the joyous Roberts did not score.

'Look here,' said Mr. Tom, addressing the company at large after she had missed an easy shot, 'she's only humbugging; she's a first-rate player; she could give any one of you thirty in a hundred and make you wish you had never been born. I say it's all humbug; she's a first-rate player. Why, she once beat me, playing even!'

But even this protest did not hinder Frank King and Edith coming out triumphant winners; and Madge did not seem at all depressed by her defeat, though she said apologetically to Mr. Roberts that one could not play one's best always.

Mr. Tom perceived that this would not do, so he fell back on pool (penny and six-penny), so that each should fight for his own hand. He himself took a ball, but, being strong and also magnanimous, would have no more than two lives.

Here, however, a strange thing happened. Frank King's ball was yellow, Madge's green, Mr. Tom's brown. Now, by some mysterious process, that yellow ball was always in a commanding position near the middle of the table, while, when Mr. Tom came to play, the green ball was as invariably under a cushion.

'Well, you *are* a sniggler, Madge,' said her brother, becoming very angry. 'You play for not a single thing but the cushion. I didn't think you cared so much for two-pence-halfpenny in coppers.'

'How can I play out when you follow?'

said Madge; but even that flattery of his skill was unavailing.

'Wait a bit,' said he; 'I'll catch you. You can't always sniggle successfully. Even Roberts himself—I beg your pardon Mr. Roberts, it was the other Roberts I meant—couldn't always get under the cushion. Wait a bit.'

There was no doubt that Madge was a most provoking and persistent sniggler. She would play for nothing, and the consequence was that Frank King, to his own intense astonishment, found himself possessed of his original three lives, while everybody else's lives were slowly dwindling down. She played with such judgment, indeed, that Mr. Tom at length got seriously angry, and began to hit wildly at the green ball in the savage hope of fluking it, the inevitable result being that he ran in himself twice, and departed from the game, and from the room too, saying he was going to smoke a cigar.

Then these four diverged into various varieties of the game, in all of which Madge was Frank King's champion and instructress; and he was very grateful to her, and tried to do his best, though he was chiefly engaged in thinking that her clear blue-gray eyes were so singularly like Nan's eyes. Indeed, Madge had now to put forth all her skill, for he and she were playing partners against the other two, and it was but little help she got from him.

'I am very sorry,' he said to her, after making a fearfully bad shot. 'I ought to apologise.'

'At all events, don't always leave the red ball over a pocket,' she said, sharply; but that may have been less temper than an evidence that she was really in earnest about the game.

Moreover, they came out victors after all, and she was greatly pleased; and she modestly disclaimed what he said about her having done all the scoring, and said she thought he played very well considering how few opportunities he must have had of practising. As she said so—looking frankly towards him—he thought that was just the way Nan would have spoken. The pleasant and refined expression of the mouth was just the same, and there was the same careless grace of the fair hair that escaped from its bonds in fascinating tangles. He thought her face was a little less freckled than Nan's—perhaps she did not brave the sunlight and the sea air so much.

The evening passed with a wonderful

rapidity; when Mr. Tom came back again into the room, followed by a servant bringing seltzer-water and things, they found it was nearly eleven.

'I must bid your mamma good-night and be off,' said Frank King to Madge.

'Oh,' she said, 'it is unnecessary; mamma goes to her room early. She will make her excuses to you to-morrow.'

In an instant the pale, pretty face had flushed up.

'I mean when you call again, if you are not going back to London at once,' she stammered.

'Oh no,' he said quite eagerly, 'I am not going back to London at once; I may stay here some little time. And, of course, I shall call and see your mamma again if I may—perhaps to-morrow.'

'Then we may see you again,' she said

pleasantly, as she offered him her hand.
'Good night ; Edith and I will leave you
to your billiards and cigars. And I hope
your prophecies are not going to interfere
with our morning walk to-morrow. When
there is a heavy sea coming in you see it
very well from the New Pier. Good-night.'

Miss Madge went upstairs to her room,
but instead of composing her mind to sleep,
she took out writing materials and wrote
this letter :

'Dear old Mother Nan—You won't
guess who is below at this moment—
11 p.m.—playing billiards with Tom and
Mr. Roberts. Captain King. If I were
he I would call myself Holford King,
for that sounds better. Edith says he is
greatly improved, and she always said
he was nice-looking. I think he is improved. He was not in uniform, of course,

which was a pity, for I remember him before; but at all events he wore neat, plain gold studs, and not a great big diamond or opal. I can't bear men wearing jewels like that; why don't they wear a string of pearls round their neck? I have been in such a fright. H. sent me a letter—not in his own handwriting. Isn't it silly? I don't want my name in the papers. Tom says they will put him in prison "like winking" if he is not careful. It is stupid; and of course I shall not answer it, or have anything to do with him. Mr. Roberts dined here this evening. I think he has too much to say for himself. I like quiet and gentlemanly men. Captain King and his party got 135 pheasants last Thursday, to say nothing of hares and rabbits; so I suppose they have good shooting. I wish they would

ask Tom.   *C. J.* has disappeared from
Brighton, so far as I can make out; and I
beleive (*sic*) he is haunting the neighbourhood of Lewes, looking out for a certain
old Mother Hubbard.   Happily he has
got nothing to fear from the Chancery
people : I suppose they daren't interfere
with the Church.   My sealskin coat has
come back; it is beautiful now, and I
have got a hat and feather exactly the
same colour as my Indian red skirt, so
I think they will go very well together.
The sealskin looks blacker than it was.
The sea is rough to-night, but I hope
to get down the Pier to-morrow morning.
Brighton is fearfully crowded just now,
and you should come away from that
sleepy old Lewes, and have a look at your
friends.   Good-night, dear Nan.

                                    ' MADGE.'

CHAPTER XIII.

THE woman is not born who can quite forget the man who has once asked her to become his wife, even though at the moment she may have rejected the offer without a thought of hesitation. Life with her, as with all of us, is so much a matter of experiment, and so rarely turns out to be what one anticipated, that even when she is married, and surrounded with children, husband, and friends, she cannot but at times bethink herself of that proposal, and wonder what would have happened if she had accepted it. Would her own life have been fuller, happier, less occupied with trivial and sordid cares? Would he have become as great and famous if she had married him, and hampered him with early ties? Might not she—supposing things to have gone the other way—have saved him from utter ruin, and have given him courage and hope? After all, there is nothing more important in the world than human happiness; and as the simple 'Yes' or 'No' of maidenhood may decide the happiness of not one but two lives, that is why it is a matter of universal interest in song and story; and that is why quite elderly people, removed by half a century from such frivolities themselves, but nevertheless possessed of memory and a little imagination, and still conscious that life has been throughout a puzzle and a game of chance, and that even in their case it might have turned out very differently, find themselves awaiting with a strange curiosity and anxiety the decision of some child of seventeen, knowing no more of the world than a baby dormouse.

On the other hand, the woman who does not marry is still less likely to forget such an offer. Here, plainly enough, was a turning-point in her life; what has happened since she owes to her decision then. And as an unmarried life is naturally and necessarily an unfulfilled life, where no great duty or purpose steps in to stop the gap, it is but little wonder if in moments of disquietude or unrest the mind should travel away in strange speculations, and if the memory of a particular person should be kept very green indeed. Nan Beresford, at the age of twenty, would

have been greatly shocked if you had told
her that during the past three years she
had been almost continually thinking about
the young sailor whom she had rejected at
Bellagio.   Had she not been most explicit
—even eagerly explicit ?   Had she not ex-
perienced an extraordinary sense of relief
when he was well away from the place, and
when she could prove to herself in close
self-examination that she was in no way to
blame for what had occurred ?   She was a
little sorry for him, it is true ; but she could
not believe that it was a very serious
matter.   He would soon forget that idle
dream in the brisk realities of his profession, and he would show that he was not
like those other young men who came
fluttering round her sisters with their sim-
mering sentimentalities and vain flirtations.
Above all, she had been explicit.   That

episode was over and closed. It was attached to Bellagio; leaving Bellagio, they would leave it also behind. And she was glad to get away from Bellagio.

Yes; Nan would have been greatly shocked if you had told her that during these three years she had been frequently thinking of Frank King—except, of course, in the way any one may think of an officer in her Majesty's Navy, whose name sometimes appears in the Admiralty appointments in the newspapers. Her mind was set on far other and higher things. It was the churches and pictures of Italy that began it—the frescoes in the cloisters, the patient sculpture, telling of the devotion of lives, even the patient needlework on the altars. She seemed to breathe the atmosphere of an Age of Faith. And when, after a long period of delightful reverie abroad,

and mystical enjoyment of music and
architecture and painting, all combining to
place their noblest gifts at the service of
religion, she returned to her familiar home
in Brighton, some vague desire still remained in her heart that she might be able
to make something beautiful of her life,
something less selfish and worldly than the
lives of most she saw around her. And it
so happened that among her friends those
who seemed to her most earnest in their
faith and most ready to help the poor and
the suffering—those who had the highest
ideals of existence and strove faithfully to
reach these—were mainly among the High
Church folk. Insensibly she drew nearer
and nearer to them. She took no interest
at all in any of the controversies then
raging about the position of the Ritualists
in the Church of England; it was persons

not principles that claimed her regard ; and
when she saw that So-and-so and So-and-
so in her own small circle of friends were
living, or striving to live, pure and noble
and self-sacrificing lives, she threw in her
lot with them, and she was warmly welcomed. For Nan was popular in a way.
All that acerbity of her younger years had
now ripened into a sort of sweet and tolerant good-humour. Tom Beresford called
her a Papist, and angrily told her to give
up 'that incense-dodge ;' but he was very
fond of her all the same, and honoured
her alone with his confidence, and would
have no one say any ill of her. Nay, for
her sake he consented to be civil to the
Rev. Mr. Jacomb.

Of Charles Jacomb it needs only be
said at present that he had recently been
transferred to an extremely High Church

at Brighton from an equally High Church
in a large, populous, and poor parish in
the south-east of London, where the semi-
Catholic services had succeeded in attract-
ing a considerable number of people, who
otherwise would probably have gone to no
church at all.   It was his description of
his work in this neighbourhood that had
won for him the respect and warm esteem
of Nan Beresford.   The work was hard.
The services were almost continuous;
there was a great deal of visitation to be
got through ; in these labours he naturally
ran against cases of distress that no human
being could withstand; and he had £60
a year.   Moreover, there were no delicate
compensations such as attend the labours
of curates in some more favoured places.
There was not—Mr. Jacomb emphatically
remarked—there was not a gentleman in

the parish. When he went to Brighton he had considerably less work, and a great deal more of dinners and society, and pleasant attentions. And Mr. Jacomb, while he was a devoted, earnest, and hard-working priest, was also an Englishman, and liked his dinner, and that was how he became acquainted with the Beresfords, and gradually grew to be an intimate friend of the family. His attentions to Nan were marked, and she knew it. She knew, although he had said nothing to her about it, that he wished her to be his wife; and though she would rather have been enabled to devote her life to some good end in some other way, was not this the only way open to her? By herself, she was so help-less to do anything. So many of her friends seemed to cultivate religion as a higher species of emotion—a sort of luxurious satisfaction that ended with themselves. Nan wanted to do something. If Mr. Jacomb had still been in the south-east of London, working on his £60 a year, Nan would have had no doubt as to what she ought to do.

But Nan had very serious doubt; more than that, she sometimes broke down, and delivered herself over to the devil. At such times a strange yearning would take possession of her; the atmosphere of exalted religious emotion in which she lived would begin to feel stifling; at all costs, she would have to get out of this hot-house, and gain a breath of brisk sea air. And then she would steal away like a guilty thing on one of her long land cruises along the coast; and she would patiently talk to the old shepherds on the downs, and wait for their laconic answers; and she

would make observations to the coastguardsmen about the weather ; and always
her eyes, which were very clear and long-
sighted, were on the outlook for Singing
Sal. Then if by some rare and happy
chance she did run across that free-and-
easy vagrant, they always had a long chat
together—Sal very respectful, the young
lady very matter-of-fact ; and generally the
talk came round to be about sailors. Nan
Beresford had got to know the rig of
every vessel that sailed the sea. Further
than that, she herself was unaware that
every morning as she opened the news-
paper she inadvertently turned first of all
to the ' Naval and Military Intelligence,'
until she had acquired an extraordinary
knowledge of the goings and comings and
foreign stations of her Majesty's ships.
And if she sometimes reflected that most

officers were transferred to home stations
for a time, or took their leave in the
ordinary way, and also that she had never
heard of Captain King—for she saw he
had been made Commander on account of
some special service—being in England,
was it not natural that she might have
a secret consciousness that she was perhaps responsible for his long banishment ?

But these solitary prowls along the
coast, and these conferences with Singing
Sal, were wrong; and she knew they were
wrong; and she went back to the calmer
atmosphere of those beautiful services in
which the commonplace, vulgar world outside was forgotten.   She grew, indeed, to
have a mysterious feeling that to her the
Rev. Charles Jacomb personified religion,
and that Singing Sal, in like manner, was
a sort of high priestess of Nature ; and that

they were in deadly antagonism. They were Ormuzd and Ahriman. She was a strangely fanciful young woman, and she dwelt much on this thing, until, half fearing certain untoward doubts and promptings of her heart, she began to think that if now and at once Mr. Jacomb would only ask her to be his wife, she would avoid all perils and confusions by directly accepting him, and so decide her future for ever.

But that morning that brought her Madge's letter saying that Captain Frank King was in Brighton, Nan was singularly disturbed. She was staying with the Rev. Mr. Clark and his wife—an old couple who liked to have their house brightened occasionally by the presence of some one of younger years. They were good people— very, very good; and a little tedious. Nan, however, was allowed considerable liberty, and was sometimes away the whole day from breakfast-time till dinner.

Madge had written her letter in a hurry; but did not post it, in her inconsequential fashion, until the afternoon of the next day, so that Nan got it on the morning of the following day. She read and re-read it; and then, somehow, she wanted to think about it in the open— under the wide skies, near the wide sea. She wanted to go out—and think. And she was a little bit terrified to find that her heart was beating fast.

She made some excuse or other after breakfast, and departed. It was a clear, beautiful December morning, the sun shining brilliantly on the evergreens and on the red houses of the bright, clean, picturesque, English-looking old town. She went down to the station, and waited

for the first train going to Newhaven.
When it came in, she took her place, and
away the train went, at no breakneck
speed, down the wide valley of the Ouse,
which, even on this cold December morning, looked pleasant and cheerful enough.
For here and there the river caught a
steely-blue light from the sky overhead;
and the sunshine shone along the round
chalk hills; and there were little patches
of villages far away among the dusk of the
leafless trees, where the church spire rising
into the blue seemed to attract the wheel-
ing of pigeons. To Nan it was all a familiar scene; she frequently spent the day
in this fashion.

Nan was now three years older than
when we last saw her at Bellagio. Perhaps
she had not grown much prettier—and she
never had great pretentions that way; but

along with the angularity, so to speak, of
her ways of thinking, she had also lost the
boniness of her figure. She was now
more fully formed, though her figure was
still slender and graceful; and she had
acquired a grave and sweet expression,
that spoke of a very kindly, humorous,
tolerant nature within. Children came to
her readily ; and she let them pull her hair.
She was incapable of a harsh judgment.
The world seemed beautiful to her ; and she
enjoyed living—especially when she was
on the high downs overlooking the sea.

This getting out into the open was on
this occasion a great relief to her. She
argued with herself. What did it matter
to her whether Frank King were in
Brighton, or even that he had been at
the house in Brunswick Terrace, dining,
and playing billiards ? He had probably

forgotten that ever he had been at Bellagio. She was glad the weather was fine. No doubt her sisters would soon be setting out for their morning stroll down the pier.

Nan had taken her ticket for Newhaven Wharf, with a vague intention of walking from thence by the short cut to Seaford, and from Seaford to Alfriston, and so back to Lewes. However, when the train stopped she thought she would have a look at the harbour, and very pretty and bright and busy it appeared on this clear morning; the brass and copper of the steamers all polished up, flags flying, the sun brilliant on the green water of the estuary and on the blue water of the ponds beyond that were ruffled with the wind. Then, just below her, came in the ferry-boat. She thought she would cross (though that was not the way to Seaford). When she got

to the other side, the slopes leading up to
the fort seemed temptingly high ; she knew
that from the summit of the downs this
morning one would have a splendid view.
And so, perhaps from mere habit, she took
the old familiar road—past the coastguard
station, past the pools of ruffled water, up
the valley by the farmstead, and so on to
the high and solitary downs overlooking
the wide, moving, shining sea.

Brighton ought to be fair and beautiful
on such a morning as this; perhaps by-
and-by she might come to have a glimpse
of the pale yellow terraces of the distant
town.   No doubt by this time Edith and
Madge were on the pier—Madge with her
red skirt and black sealskin coat.   Madge
always dressed smartly—perhaps even a
trifle boldly.   The band would be playing
now.   In the sheltered places it would be

almost warm; there you could sit down and talk and watch the ships go by. She supposed that in course of time they would go back for luncheon. That was always a merry meal at home. They generally had visitors whom they had met casually—on the pier, or in the King's Road.

So Nan was thinking and dreaming as she walked idly along, when her attention was suddenly arrested by a sound as of music. She looked round; there was no human being in sight; and the telegraph wires, which sometimes deceived the ear, were far too far away. Then as she went on again, she discovered whence the sound proceeded—from a little wooden hut facing the sea, which had probably been erected there as a shelter for the coastguardsmen. As she drew nearer, she recognised the staccato twanging of a guitar; so she made sure this was Singing Sal. She drew nearer still—her footsteps unheard on the smooth turf—and then she discovered that Sal was singing away to herself, not for amusement, as was her wont, but for practice. There were continual repetitions. Nan got quite close to the hut, and listened.

Singing Sal was doing her very best. She was singing with very great effect; and she had a hard, clear voice that could make itself heard, if it was not of very fine quality. But what struck Nan was the clever fashion in which this woman was imitating the Newcastle burr. It was a pitman's song, with a refrain something like this—

> *Ho thy way*,[1] my bonnie bairn,
> *Ho thy way*, upon my airm,
> *Ho thy way*, thou still may learn
>   To say Dada sae bonnie.

[1] A corruption, I am told, of 'haud thy way'—'hold on thy way.' The song is a common one in the North of England.

It was very clear that Sal was proud of her performance; and she had a good right to be, for she had caught the guttural accent to perfection. For the rest it was an instructive song to be sung as a lullaby to a child; for this was what Nan more or less made out amid the various experiments and repetitions :—

> Oh, Johnnie is a clever lad ;
> Last neet he fuddled all he had ;
> This morn he wasna very bad ;
>   He looked the best of ony !
>
> When Johnnie's drunk he'll tak a knife,
> And threaten sair to hae my life :
> Wha wadna be a pitman's wife,
>   To hae a lad like Johnnie !
>
> Yonder's Johnnie coming noo ;
> He looks the best of a' the crew !
> They've all gone to the barley moo,
>   To hae a glass wi' Johnnie.
>
> So let's go get the bacon fried,
> And let us mak a clean fireside,

And when he comes he will thee ride
      Upon his knee sae cannie.
Ho thy way, my bonnie bairn,
Ho thy way, upon my airm,
Ho thy way, thou still may learn
      To say Dada sae bonnie !

But this was likely to go on for ever; so Nan quietly stepped round to the door of the hut, where she found Singing Sal sitting on the little cross bench, entirely occupied with her guitar and the new song. When she looked up, on finding the door darkened, she did not scream; her nerves were not excitable.

'Oh, dear me, is it you, Miss?' she said. 'No wonder I did not hear ye; for I was making enough noise myself. I hope you are very well, Miss; it is many a day since I have seen you on the downs.'

'I have been living in Lewes for some time,' said Nan. 'I have been listening to the song you were singing. That is not the kind of song that sailors like, is it ?'

So they had begun about sailors again ; and the good genius Ormuzd was clean forgotten.

CHAPTER XIV.

AT HOME.

ALL that night, as Frank King had feared,
a heavy gale from the south-west raged
furiously; the wind shaking the houses
with violent gusts; the sea thundering
along the beach. But in the morning,
when Brighton awoke, it found that the
worst of the storm had passed over, leaving
only a disturbed and dangerous look about
the elements, and also a singular clearness
in the air, so that the low hard colours
of water and land and sky were strangely
intense and vivid. Near the shore the sea

had been beaten into a muddy brown; then that melted into a cold green farther out; and that again deepened and deepened until it was lost in a narrow line of ominous purple, black just where the sea met the vague and vaporous gray sky. In fact, at this moment, the seaward view from any Brighton window resembled nothing so much as an attempt at water-colour that a schoolgirl has got into a hopeless mess through washing and washing away at her skies, until she has got her heaviest colour smudged over the horizon-line.

But then that was only temporary. Every few minutes another change would steal over this strange, shifting, clear, dark world. Sometimes a long streak of sunny green—as sharp as the edge of a knife— far out at sea told that there was some unseen rift declaring itself overhead in

that watery sky. Then a pale grayness
would come up from the south-west and
slowly cover over Worthing as with a veil;
and then again that could be seen to go
trailing away inland, and the long spur
beyond the bay appear blacker than ever.
Sometimes too, as if in contrast with all
these cold hard tones and colours, a wonder
of light would slowly concentrate on the
far cliffs in the east, until Seaford Head
became a mass of glorified golden white,
hung apparently between sea and sky.
Altogether, it was not a day to tempt
fashionable folk to go out for their accus-
tomed promenade; and assuredly it was
not a day, supposing them bent on going
out, to suggest that they should be too
elaborate about their costume.

Nevertheless, when Miss Madge Beresford came into the billiard-room, where

her brother was patiently practising the spot stroke, her appearance seemed to produce a great effect.

'Well, we *have* got on a swagger dress this time!' cried Mr. Tom, who, though he had never been to Oxford, was a genuine free-trader in slang, and was ready to import it from anywhere.

He stared at her—at her dark Indian-red hat and skirt, and her long tight-fitting black sealskin coat—and she bore the scrutiny patiently.

'You are not going out on a morning like this?' he said, at length.

'There is no rain now; and the streets are quite dry,' pleaded Madge. 'I know it's going to be fine.'

'It's no use, Baby. There won't be a soul to admire your new dress. Better go and finish those slippers for me.'

He proceeded with his billiards.

'Won't you come, Tom?' she said. I went to the bazaar with you, when you wanted to see Kate Harman.'

'Wanted to see Kate Harman?' he said, contemptuously. 'Couldn't anybody see Kate Harman who paid half-a-crown at the door?'

'But I took you up and introduced you to her.'

'Introduced me to her! What introduction do you need at a stall at a bazaar, except to pay a couple of sovereigns for a shilling's worth of scent? Who told you I wanted to speak to Kate Harman? I'll tell you what it is, Baby; it's very unlady-like to impute motives.'

'I never did anything of the kind,' said his sister, hotly. 'Never.'

She did not quite understand what

accusation had been brought against her; but she did not like the sound of the word 'unladylike.'

'Very well,' said he, laying down his cue, 'since you say I am incapable of speaking the truth, I suppose I must go and walk up and down the pier with you. There's one thing sure : *I* shan't be stared at.'

So he went and got his hat and cane and gloves, and when he had buttoned himself all over into the smallest possible compass, he called for his sister, and together they went out into the gusty, clear, sea-scented morning.

They had the spacious thoroughfare nearly to themselves, though the pavements were fairly dry now. For the day was wild-looking still, the occasional gleam of sunlight was spectral and watery, and a black shadow melting into a soft gray told

of showers falling far away at sea. At a
great many drawing-room windows, coffee-
room windows, club windows, were people
standing, their hands behind their back,
apparently uncertain whether or not to
venture out. And no doubt some of these,
remarking Tom and Madge Beresford
pass, must have thought they formed a
very handsome couple—the tall, well-built
young fellow who looked three-and-twenty,
though he was not so much, and the pretty
girl of eighteen who also had a good figure
and walked well. Their features were
much alike too ; most would have guessed
them to be brother and sister.

'I observe,' remarked Mr. Tom, pro-
foundly, as he gazed with admiration at
his own boots, 'that when I come out with
you, Baby, I have to do all the talking.
When I go out with Nan, now, she does it

all and I am amused. It isn't that I am selfish ; but a girl come to your time of life —a woman indeed—ought to cultivate the art of amusing people. There is a want of originality about you——'

'There is a want of politeness about you,' said Miss Madge, calmly.

'There is not that flow of ideas that helps one to pass the time. Now that ought to be the business of women. Men who have the hard work of the world to get through require to be entertained, and women should make a study of it, and learn to be amusing——'

'You won't talk like that to your rich widow,' said his sister, 'when you have to go to her for a cheque.'

'Now, there's what I would call a sort of vacuity in your mind,' he continued, bending his cane from time to time on the pavement, 'that might be filled up with something. You might read the newspapers. You might get to know that a Conservative Government and a Liberal Government are not in office at the same time—not generally, at least.'

'Tom,' she said, 'do you think you could get Captain King to come to the Hunt ball?'

He glanced at her suspiciously.

'Captain King?' said he. 'How do you know I am going to see Captain King again? How do you know that he did not go back to town this morning?'

'Because,' she answered, with her eyes fixed on some distant object, 'because I can see him on the pier.'

Tom Beresford had a quick, dark suspicion that he had been made a fool of, even while he was lecturing his sister on her ignorance; but he was not going to admit anything of the kind.

'Yes,' he said, carelessly, 'I fancy that is King coming along. I hope he won't be gone before we get there; I want him to tell me where he gets his boots. Mine aren't bad, you know,' he said, glancing approvingly at these important objects, 'but there's a style about his that I rather fancy.'

'Don't forget about the ball, Tom,' said his sister; 'it would be very nice if we could get up a little party amongst ourselves.'

But Tom, as he walked along, continued to glance down at his glazed boots in a thoughtful and preoccupied manner; it was clear that his mind was charged concerning them.

Frank King was on the pier, and very few others besides, except the musicians in their box. He threw away a cigar, and came forward quickly. His face expressed much pleasure, though he regarded Madge Beresford with something of timidity.

'I was afraid you would not venture out on such a morning,' he said, looking at the clear blue-gray eyes that were immediately turned away.

Her manner was civil, but that was all. She shook hands with him, of course, and regarded him for half a second; but then she turned aside somewhat, so that he and Tom might talk together. For he was Mr. Tom's friend, and no doubt they might have something to say to each other about boots or cigars, or such things.

However, the three of them very soon found themselves walking together, up towards the end of the empty Pier, and Tom was in an amazingly good humour, and

did his best to amuse this new friend.
They sat down where they were sheltered
from the gusts of wind, and listened a little
to the music, and talked a great deal—
though Madge chiefly listened. Madge
pretended to be mostly interested in the
music, and in the few more people who
had now been tempted to come down the
pier; but she knew that while her brother
and Captain King were very busy talking,
the latter was very frequently regarding
her. What she did not know was that he
was trying to make himself believe that
that was Nan who was sitting there.

Then they went for a stroll again, and
they looked at the kiosques, and they took
refuge from a few passing drops of rain;
and they hurried to see a heavy fishing-
smack go by the end of the pier, beating
out against the south-westerly wind. And

although Frank King again and again addressed her, as was demanded of him, she did not enter much into conversation with him. He was Tom's friend, she let it be understood. Nevertheless, she met his eyes once or twice, and she had a pleasant and amiable look.

She began to think that there must be something very striking and attractive about this young sailor, when even her brother Tom—who seemed to consider that the whole world should wait upon his highness—so clearly went out of his way to make himself agreeable. Not only that, but when they had had enough of the pier, and had taken a stroll or two along the King's Road, bringing the time to nearly one o'clock, what must Mr. Tom do but insist that Frank King should come in and lunch with them?

'Well, I will,' said he, 'if you will dine with me at the hotel in the evening. Dining by yourself at a hotel is not exhilarating.'

'But you'd far better dine with us too,' said Mr. Tom, boldly.

'Oh, I can't do that,' said Frank King —but with a slight increase of colour, which showed that he wished he could. 'Even as it is, I am afraid Lady Beresford will think it rather cool if I turn up again now.'

'Oh, you don't know what Brighton is at this time of year,' said Mr. Tom. 'All the resident people like ourselves keep open house, don't you know? and very glad to. We never know how many are coming in to lunch; but then they put up with anything; and it's great fun; it's an occupation for idle people. Then, when

you've got a billiard-table, they can turn
to that on wet days. Or Edith can give
them some music; they say she's rather
a swell at it. You see, everybody is in
Brighton in December, with friends or in
hotels; and, as I say, it's a case of open
house and take your chance.'

'We are more formal, and a little duller,
in Wiltshire,' said Frank King. 'I wish
you'd come to Kingscourt for a few days.
We haven't shot the best of the covers
yet.'

Those who thought that Tom Beresford
was a foolish youth knew nothing about
him. Without a hum or a ha he said—

'Yes, I will. When?'

'I'm going back for Christmas. Of
course you'll have to stay here with your
sisters. As soon after that as you can
manage.'

'I could come to you on the 27th or 28th.'

'That's settled, then. I will write and let you know about trains and things.'

As luck, good or ill, would have it, there was no other visitor at lunch; the party consisting of Lady Beresford, her two daughters, Mr. Tom, and Captain Frank King. But Mr. Tom was in high spirits over this prospective visit to Kingscourt, and was most amiable to everybody and everthing; he even said that he himself would go through to Lewes and fetch Nan home for Christmas.

Now this was odd: that, whenever Nan's name was mentioned, Frank King always glanced up with a quick look, as if he were surprised. Was he beginning to believe, then, as he had tried to make himself believe, that this was the real Nan

Beresford now on the other side of the table? Was he surprised to be reminded of the other Nan far away—and now no doubt greatly altered from her former self? Madge Beresford was aware that her neighbour opposite regarded her very frequently—and she pretended not to be conscious of it; but once or twice, when she looked up and her eyes met his, she thought there was an oddly wistful or even puzzled expression in those dark blue eyes that Edith was always talking about.

After luncheon Lady Beresford retired to her room, as was her wont; the two young ladies went upstairs to the drawing-room, and Captain King accompanied them, for Madge had asked him to advise her about the rigging of some boats she had been sketching. Mr. Tom remained below to practise the spot stroke.

In the drawing-room Miss Edith hoped that her playing a little would not interfere with their artistic pursuits; and Madge went and got her sketch-book and water-colours, and carried them to a small table at one of the windows, and sat down. Captain King remained standing.

The sketches, to tell the truth, were as bad as bad could be. They were all experimental things, done out of her own head, aiming at a land of the beautiful, unknown to anybody on earth but the chromo-lithographer. The actual sea was out there, staring her in the face, and there were boats on the beach and boats on the water; but instead of trying her hand at anything before her, she must needs imagine lovely pictures, mostly of blue and pink, with goats perched on brown crags, and an ill-drawn eagle soaring over an Alpine peak. There were, however, one or two sketches of mist or moonlight or thunderstorm that had certainly a weird and eerie effect; but it was not necessary to tell the spectator that these had been got in moments of impatience when, after laborious trials at brilliant-hued scenes, the angry artist had taken up a big brush and washed the whole thing into chaos—thereby, to her astonishment, reaching something, she did not know exactly what, that was at all events mysterious and harmonious in tone.

But it was the shipping about which she had sought his advice. The little white dots on blue lakes that were supposed to be feluccas or barchettas he passed; but when it came to a big sailing-boat lying on a beach, and that beach presumably Cornish, from the colour of the rocks, he made a civil and even timid remonstrance.

'I don't think I would have the mast quite in the middle of the boat, if I were you,' said he, gently.

'I thought it always was,' she said— and yet if she had gone to the window she might have seen.

'If it is a lugger, you see,' he continued, giving her all sorts of chances of escape, 'the mast would be at the bow. And if it is a cutter, you would still have to put the mast farther forward, and give her a boom and a bowsprit. Or if it is a yawl, then you would have a little jigger-mast astern—about there——'

'Oh, I can't be expected to know things like that,' she said. 'Scientific accuracy isn't wanted. They're only sketches.'

'Yes; oh yes,' he said.

'Won't that boat do?' she demanded.

'Oh yes, it will do,' he said, fearful of offending her. 'It isn't exactly where they put masts, you know; but then few people know about boats or care about them.'

She was not very well pleased; but she continued to show him more sketches, until Mr. Tom came up to see when they were coming to billiards.

'I shouldn't have shown you these at all,' she said. 'I don't take interest in them myself. I would far rather draw and paint flowers; but we never have any flowers now except those waxen-looking heaths and that flaming pointsettia over there.'

'What did you call it, Madge?' said Mr. Tom.

'I called it pointsettia,' she said, with dignity.

'Gamekeeper's Greek, I should say,' he remarked, with his hands in his pockets. 'A cross between a pointer and a setter. You shouldn't use long words, Madge. Come along down.'

But this mention of flowers put a new idea into the head of Captain Frank King. That very morning he had passed a window where he had seen all sorts of beautiful blossoms, many of them lying in cotton wool—pink and white camellias, white hyacinths, scarlet geraniums, lilies of the valley, and what not. Now might he not be permitted to send Miss Margaret a selection of these rare blossoms—not as a formal bouquet at all, but merely for the purposes of painting? They would simply be materials for an artist; and they would look well in a pretty basket, on a soft cushion of wool.

CHAPTER XV.

A MESSAGE.

FRANK KING could never exactly define
what peculiarities of mind, or person, or
manner it was that had so singularly attracted him in Nan Beresford, though he
had spent many a meditative hour on
board ship in thinking about her. In any
case, that boyish fancy was one that a
few years' absence might very well have
been expected to cure. But the very
opposite had happened. Perhaps it was
the mere hopelessness of the thing that
made him brood the more over it, until it

took possession of his life altogether. He
kept resolutely abroad, so that he had but
few chances of falling in love with somebody else, which is the usual remedy in
such cases. When at length he was
summoned home, about the first news
that reached him was of Nan's contem-
plated marriage. He was not surprised.
And when he consented to go down to
Brighton with her brother, it was that
he might have just one more glimpse of
one whom he always had known was lost
to him. He had nothing to reproach her
or himself with. It was all a misfortune,
and nothing more. But his life had been
changed for him by that mere boyish
fancy.

Then came that wonderful new hope.
Nan was away; Nan was impossible; but
here was the very counterpart of Nan;

and why should he not transfer all that
lingering love and admiration from the
one sister to the other who so closely resembled her? It was the prompting of
despair as much as anything else. He
argued with himself. He tried to make
himself believe that this was really Nan—
only grown a year or so older than the
Nan whom he had last seen at Como. Of
course there must be differences; people
changed with the changing years. Sometimes he turned away, so that he might
only hear her; and her voice was like
Nan's.

Now, if Frank King was busy per-
suading himself that this transference of
affection was not only natural and possible,
but indeed the easiest and simplest thing
in the world, it must be admitted that he
obtained every help and encouragement

from Madge Beresford herself. She was more than kind to him; she was attentive; she professed great respect for his opinions; and she did her best to conceal—or rather let us say subdue—her bad temper. And they were very much together during these two or three days. Frank King, being on such intimate terms of friendship with Mr. Tom, had almost become an inmate of the house. His being carried off to lunch, when they met him in the morning, was a matter of course. Then he watched Madge paint, and listened to Edith's music; or they all went downstairs and played billiards, and by that time it was the hour for the afternoon promenade. It was no matter to them that December afternoons are short, and sometimes cold; one's health must be preserved despite the weather; and then again, Brighton looked

very picturesque in the gathering dusk,
with the long rows of her golden lamps.
To observe this properly, however, you
ought to go out on the Pier; and although
at that hour at that time of the year there
is not a human being to be found there,
that need not interfere with your apprecia-
tion of the golden-lit spectacle.

Moreover, Mr. Tom was a tyrant.
When he had settled that Captain King
might as well remain to dinner, instead
of going away to dine by himself at his
hotel, it was no use for Captain King to
resist. And then Tom's invitation, for
mere courtesy sake, had to be repeated
by Lady Beresford, and prettily seconded
by the two girls. No such favours, be it
observed, were showered on the effer-
vescent Roberts or on young Thynne:
Mr. Tom had taken the sailor suitor under

his protection; there was to be a distinction drawn.

One night, just after Frank King had left, Tom and his sister were by themselves in the billiard-room.

'I want to speak to you, Madge,' said he, in a tone that meant something serious.

'Very well, then.'

'Now, none of your airs and pretence,' he said. 'You needn't try to gammon me.'

'If you would talk English, one might understand you,' she said, spitefully.

'You understand me well enough. When you were on the Pier this morning your eyes were just as wide open as anybody's. And again this afternoon, when you were up on the Marine Parade.'

Madge flushed a little, but said nothing.

'You know as well as anybody that that fellow Hanbury is hanging about.'

said Tom, regarding her with suspicion. 'He is always loitering round, dodging after you. And I won't have it. I'll write to the Chief Clerk if he doesn't mind.'

'I don't suppose the Chief Clerk and the Vice Chancellor and the whole lot of them,' said Madge, pretending to be much interested in the tip of her cue, 'can expel a person from Brighton who is doing no harm.'

'Doing no harm? If you didn't encourage him, do you think he'd hang about like that? If he knew distinctly you wanted him to be off, do you think he'd spend his time slinking about the streets? I believe he has been writing to you again.'

This was quite a random shot, but it told.

'He sent me one letter—not in his own handwriting,'. Madge confessed, diffidently.

'Show it to me!'

'I can't. I burned it. I was afraid. Tom, you wouldn't get the poor fellow into trouble!'

'I've no patience with you!' he said angrily. 'Why can't you be fair and aboveboard? Why don't you send the fellow about his business at once——'

'Well, I have.'

'Why don't you settle the thing straight? You know Frank King wants to marry you: anybody can see that. Why don't you have him, and be done with it?'

Madge turned away a little, and said with a very pretty smile,

'And so I would, if he would ask me.'

Well, Mr. Tom thought he knew something of the ways of womankind, from having been brought up among so many;

but this fairly took his breath away. He stared at her. He laid down his cue.

'Well, I'm smashed,' he said at length. And then he added slowly, 'I'm glad I've got nothing to do with you women. I believe you'd roast any fellow alive, and then cut him into bits for fourpence-halfpenny. It isn't more than three months since you were crying your eyes out about that fellow Hanbury——'

'You were as anxious as any one he should be sent away,' retorted Madge. 'It appears I can't please every one. Perhaps, on the whole, it would be as well to continue the game, for I only want three to be out.'

Tom gave up. He continued the game, and played so savagely and so well that poor Madge never got her three. And he did not recur to that subject except to say the last thing at night, as the girls were leaving—

'Look here, Madge, that fellow Hanbury had better take care.'

'I suppose he can look after himself,' said Madge. 'I have nothing to do with him. Only you can't expect me not to be sorry for him. And how am I to send him away when I dare not speak to him? And do you think the streets of Brighton belong to me?'

Tom again gave up, but was more convinced than ever that women were strange creatures, who could not be straightforward even when they tried. From that and similar generalisations, however, he invariably excepted Nan. Nan did not belong to womankind as considered as a section of the human race. Nan was Nan.

The next afternoon Captain King

called to say good-bye. He found the girls very busy over Christmas cards. Madge was painting little studies of flowers for exceptionally favoured people, and she invited him to look over these.

'They are very pretty,' he said. 'I hope the people who are fortunate enough to get them will value them. I mean they are not like ordinary Christmas cards.'

'Oh. if you like them,' said Madge, modestly, 'you might take one for yourself.'

'May I?' he said, regarding her, 'and may I choose the one?'

'Oh yes, certainly,' she answered.

'I know the one I should like to take,' he said, still regarding her. 'This one.'

It was a little bit of forget-me-not, very nicely painted—from memory. He showed it to her.

'May I take this one with me?' he said.

'Yes,' she answered, in a very low voice, and with her eyes cast down.

After that there was a brief silence, only broken by the sound of Miss Edith's pen, that young lady being at the other side of the table addressing envelopes.

Captain Frank went back to Wiltshire, greatly treasuring that bit of cardboard, and making it the basis of many audacious guesses at the future. Nan came home from Lewes for Christmas; and Madge was particularly affectionate towards her.

'What pretty flowers you have!' Nan said, just after she had arrived—the first time, indeed, she went into the dining-room.

'Yes,' Madge answered, 'Captain King sent me flowers once or twice, and some of them have kept very well. But I wish they wouldn't wire them.'

Nan turned away quickly towards the window, and said nothing.

Then Tom went down to Wiltshire, and was most warmly received at Kingscourt. Also pretty Mary Coventry, who was still staying in the house, was kind to this handsome, conceited boy; and he was rather smitten; but he kept a tight hold on himself. 'No,' he said to himself, 'I'm not going to marry any woman; I know too much about them.'

He had a royal time of it altogether; but most of all he enjoyed the quieter days, when he and Frank King went shooting rabbits on the heath. It was sharp, brisk work in the cold weather, better than standing in wet ploughed fields outside woods and waiting until both toes and fingers got benumbed. There was no formality in this business, and no ladies

turning up at lunch, and no heart-breaking
when one missed. Frank King was
excessively kind to him. Not caring very
much for shooting himself, he was content
to become Mr. Tom's henchman; and they
got on very well together. Further, in the
smoking-room at night these two were
thrown on each other's conversation—for
old Mr. King did not smoke—and it was
remarkable how interesting Captain King
found his friend's talk. It was mostly
about Madge and her sisters; and Frank
King listened eagerly, and always would
have Mr. Tom have another cigarette,
while he was busy drawing imaginative
pictures, and convincing himself more and
more that Madge was no other than Nan,
and that life had begun again for him, with
all sorts of beautiful possibilities in it. For
he could not be blind to the marked favour

that the young lady had shown him; and
he had long ceased to have any fear of the
shadowy Hanbury who was skulking somewhere unregarded in the background.

At length one night Captain Frank, in a
burst of confidence, told Mr. Tom all about
it, and asked him to say honestly what he
thought the chances were. Would Lady
Beresford have any objection? Would
Miss Margaret consider he had not known
her sufficiently long or intimately? What
was Mr. Tom's own opinion?

Mr. Tom flushed uneasily.

'I—well, you see—I keep out of that
kind of thing as a rule. Women have
such confounded queer ways. You're sure
to put your foot into it if you intermeddle.
These girls are always worrying people
about their sweethearts—all but Nan.   I
wish to goodness they were all married;

my life is made a burden to me amongst them.'

'But what do you think, Beresford? Haven't you any opinion? What would you do in a similar case?'

'I?' said Mr. Tom, with a laugh, 'I suppose I should ask the girl; and if she didn't like to say yes, she could do the other thing.'

'But—do you think there would be a chance?'

'Write and see,' said Mr. Tom, with another laugh; further than that he would not interfere.

Frank King considered for a time; and at last boldly determined to act on this advice. He sat up late that night, concocting a skilful, cautious, appealing letter; and as he re-wrote it carefully, all by himself, in the silence, it seemed to him almost as if he were beseeching Nan to reconsider the verdict she had given at Bellagio more than three years before. Life would begin all over again if only she would say yes. Sometimes he found himself thinking of that ball in Spring Gardens; and of her startled shyness, and of her winning confidence, and anxious wish to please; until he recollected that it was Madge to whom he was writing, and that Madge had never been to the ball at all.

This fateful missive was left to be despatched the first thing in the morning; and at the very least there must needs be two or three days' interval. But it cannot be said that he passed this time in terrible anxiety. He was secretly hopeful; so much so that he had begged Mr. Tom, who ought to have gone back before this time, to wait another day or so. His private reason was that he hoped to accompany Madge's brother to Brighton.

All the same, the crisis of a man's life cannot approach without causing some mental disturbance, even in the most hopeful. Long before the Kingscourt family had assembled round the breakfast-table, Frank King had ridden over, on these two or three cold mornings, to the postal town, which was nearly two miles off, so that he should not have to wait for the arrival of the bag. And at last came a letter with the Brighton postmark. He glanced at the handwriting, and thought it was Madge's. That was enough. He put it in his pocket without opening it; went out and got on his horse; and went well outside the little town into the quietude of the lanes before putting his hand into his pocket again and taking the letter out.

No, he was not very apprehensive about the result, or he could not have carried the letter thus far unopened. But all the same the contents surprised him. He had expected, at the worst, some mild refusal on the ground of haste; and, at the best, an evasive hint that he might come to Brighton and talk to Lady Beresford. But all the writing on this sheet of paper consisted of two words, '*From Madge;*' and what accompanied them was a bit of forget-me-not—not painted, this time, but a bit of the real flower. It was a pretty notion. It confessed much, without saying much. There was a sort of maiden reticence about it, and yet kindness, and hope. What Frank King did not know was this—that it was Nan Beresford who had suggested that answer to his letter.

He never knew how he got home that

morning. He was all in a tempest of eagerness and delight; he scarcely lived in to-day—it was next day. It was the future that seemed to be around him. He burst into his friend's bed-room before the breakfast gong had sounded.

' Beresford, I'll go with you whenever you like now. Whenever you like. I'm going to Brighton with you, I mean.'

' Oh, that's it, is it?' said Mr. Tom, without looking up—he was tying his shoes.

' I've heard from your sister, you know——'

' I thought so. It's all right then, is it?'

' I hope so. I'm very glad it's settled. And you know I don't want to turn you out of the house; but you've been very kind, waiting a day or two longer; and I *should* like to get to Brighton at once.'

' I'll start in five minutes if you like,'

said Mr. Tom, coolly, having finished with his shoes. 'And I suppose I ought to congratulate you. Well, I do. She's a very good sort of girl. Only——'

He hesitated. It was inauspicious.

'What do you mean?' said Captain Frank.

'Well, I've seen a good deal about women and their goings on, don't you know?' said Mr. Tom, with a sort of shrug. 'They're always changing and chopping and twisting about. The best way is to marry them offhand, and take the non-sense out of them.'

Captain Frank laughed. This was not at all alarming. And when it became secretly known that Captain Frank was immediately going to Brighton to secure his promised bride, there was a great, though discreet rejoicing at Kingscourt;

and even pretty Mary Coventry came with her demure and laughing congratulations; and Mr. Tom was made more of than ever during the few hours longer that he remained in the house. Frank King had not time to think about Nan now; it was Madge Beresford who had sent him that bit of forget-me-not.

CHAPTER XVI.

REVERIES.

No sooner had Nan come back to Brighton again, and been installed once more in her former position, than the whole house seemed to be pervaded by a quite new sense of satisfaction, the cause of which was not even guessed at. The wheels of the domestic machinery worked far more smoothly; even the servants seemed to partake of the general brightness and cheerfulness. Edith, the stupid sister, put it down to the Christmas-time, and congratulated herself on her evergreens on the walls. Mr. Tom observed that the house was far better managed when Nan was at home : that meant that he found his slippers when he wanted them, and that there was always a taper on the chimney-piece in the billiard-room. Lady Beresford had all her little whims attended to; and as for Madge, that young lady was greatly delighted to have a safe and sure confidante. For she was much exercised at this time both with her fears about Mr. Hanbury, who followed her about like a ghost, kept silent by the dread of Vice-Chancellors and tipstaffs, and her vain little hopes about Captain Frank King, whose intentions were scarcely a matter of doubt. Nan listened in her grave, sweet way that had earned for her, from Madge, the name of 'Old Mother Nan;' and then would say some nice thing to her sister; and then would carry her away on some charitable enterprise.

For this was the Christmas time; and what with continual choral services, and evergreens, and unearthly music in the still cold nights, there was a sort of exaltation in the air; and Nan wished to be practical. In consequence, Lady Beresford was gravely oppressed.

'I do believe, Nan,' she said, vexedly, one morning as she was writing out a cheque—'I do believe your only notion of Christianity is the giving away coals.'

'And a very good notion too,' said Tom, who would allow no one to say anything against Nan.

But then came that fateful letter from Frank King. It arrived on a January morning—on a clear and brilliant forenoon. just as Nan and her younger sister were

going out for a walk, tempted by the sunlight and the colours of the sea. Madge
herself took it from the postman at the
door; glanced at the address, hastily
opened the envelope, and guessed at,
rather than read, the contents.

'Oh, Nan,' she said hurriedly, 'wait a
moment. There is something—something
I want to speak to you about—come into
the dining-room—oh, do you know what
this is, Nan?—Captain King has written.'

'Yes, dear,' said Nan, calmly and
kindly, as she followed her into the empty
dining-room.

'I must not show you the letter, must
I?' said the younger sister, eagerly, though
she was herself still reading and re-reading
it. 'But you know what it is, Nan. And
I must send an answer—oh dear, what
shall I do?'

'You ought to know, Madge,' her sister said. 'You were not unprepared, surely. I thought you expected it. I thought you would have had your mind made up.'

'But it is so dreadful—so sudden—so terrible! Look at my hands—I am all shaking. Oh, Nan, what would you do— what would you do if you were me?'

Nan seemed to be thinking of something far away; it was after a second that she recalled herself to this question, and then she answered with some astonishment—

'Don't you know your own mind, Madge?'

'Well, I do in a way,' said the younger sister, still staring at the letter. 'I like him well enough. I think it would do very well; and there would be no trouble with any one. I am sorry for that poor fellow Hanbury ; but what *is* the use of his hanging about, and keeping one nervous ? There is no use in it all— nothing but bother. And I know Captain King is very fond of me, and I think he would be very kind ; and you know he is not going to sea again. And mamma would be pleased. Do you think I should go to her now ? '

' What is the use of going to any one until you know what your mind is ? '

If the unhappy Hanbury could only have seen his sweetheart at this moment— staring blankly at the open letter, with a doubt on her face which was most prob- ably inspired by some vague and tender recollection of himself ! What might not have happened if only he could have inter- vened at this crisis, and appealed to her with eyes and speech, and implored her to defy these terrible authorities in London? But Madge kept looking at the letter; and then she shut it together; and then she said with decision—

'I think it's the best thing I can do. Wait a minute, Nan; I'll go and tell mamma.'

When she came downstairs again she was quite radiant and eager in her joy.

'Oh, I'm so glad it's all settled and over. I'm so glad there'll be no more worry and bother. And really Captain King is one of the nicest-looking men we know—Edith has always said so—and he is so quiet and pleasant in his manner, and very amusing too : that is because he has no pretence. And grateful for small kindnesses ; I suppose being so long at sea, and not seeing so many people, he hasn't got *blasé*. Then he never pretends to be

bored—but why are you so solemn, Nan;
doesn't it please you?'

Nan kissed her sister.

'I hope you will be very happy, dear,'
she said, in her grave, kind way.

'Then I suppose I must answer his letter
at once,' continued Madge, in her excited
way. 'But how am I to do it, Nan?
See how my fingers are all shaking; I
couldn't write. And it would take me a
month to find out what to say—and here
you are being kept in, when you are always
wanting to be out in the open air——'

'Oh, don't mind me, Madge. I will
stay in with pleasure, if you want me.'

'But you shan't stay in on my account,
dear Mother Nan—not a bit of it—not for
all the men in the world. And yet I ought
to send him a message. I ought to write.'

'I think, Madge,' the elder sister said,

slowly, 'if that is any trouble to you, you might send him a message he would understand, without your writing much—a flower, perhaps——'

'But what sort of flower?' said the younger sister, eagerly.

Nan's face flushed somewhat, and she seemed embarrassed and slow to answer.

'You—you should know yourself,' she said, turning her eyes aside. 'Any flower, perhaps—a bit of—of forget-me-not——'

'Of course that would do very well; but where could you get forget-me-nots just now?'

Nan again hesitated; she seemed to be forcing herself to speak.

'There's a little bit in a button-hole in ——'s window,' she said, at last; 'I saw it there yesterday at least.'

'Dear Mother Nan,' said Madge, enthusiastically, 'you are as clever as twenty Vice-Chancellors! We will walk along at once, and see if it is still there. And in the meantime I will write a word on a sheet of paper—I can manage that anyway—and you might address an envelope——'

'Oh no, I couldn't do that,' said Nan, inadvertently shrinking back.

'Very well, I will struggle through it,' said Madge, blithely; and she went and got writing-materials, and scrawled the few words necessary.

They went out into the beautiful clear cold morning, and walked along through the crowd of promenaders with their fresh-coloured faces and furs telling of the wintry weather. And in due course of time they arrived at the florist's window, and found the bit of forget-me-not still in the little nosegay. Madge made no secret of her intention. She opened up the nosegay on the counter of the shop; took out the piece of forget-me-not; put it in the folded sheet of paper; and then carefully —but with fingers no longer trembling— closed the envelope. When they had come out again, and gone and posted the letter, they found themselves at a standstill.

'Now I know you would like a longer walk, Nan,' said the younger sister, 'and I am sure you won't mind if I go back at once. I do so want to write a long letter to Mary. And I haven't told Edith yet, you know.'

To this also Nan consented; and so Madge departed. Nan, left to herself, looked for a moment or two, somewhat wistfully, at the far breadths of the shining water; and then turned and walked slowly and thoughtfully along one of the wider thoroughfares leading up from the sea. The world seemed too bright and eager and busy out here; she wished to be alone, and in the dusk; and in this thoroughfare there was a church, spacious and gloomy, that was kept open all the week round. Half unconsciously to herself she walked in that direction. So absorbed was she that, when she reached the entrance, she scarcely perceived that there were some persons standing about. From the clear light of the sun she passed into a long covered way that was almost dark; there was a low sound of music issuing from the building; it was a refuge she was seeking; and she vaguely hoped that there would be few people within.

But just as she gained the entrance proper, and was about to enter the dark and dusky place before her, behold! here was a great smiling throng coming along the aisle, headed by a bridegroom and a white-clothed bride. The music that was gaily pealing through the building was the 'Wedding March' that no familiarity robs of its majestic swing and melody. Nan had suddenly a sort of guilty self-consciousness. She felt she had no business even to look on at bridal processions. She passed in by another door—into that space of dark and empty pews; and very soon the bridal people were all gone from the place, and apparently no one was left but the white-surpliced performers at the organ in the choir.

That choir was a beautiful thing away beyond the dusk. The sunlight entering by the stained-glass windows filled it with a softly golden glory; so that the

splendours of the altar, and the tall
brass candlesticks, and the seven swinging lamps, and the organ itself, were all
suffused with it, and seemed to belong to
some other world far away. And then,
after the 'Wedding March' was over,
there was a pause of silence, and a slight
sound of feet in the echoing building behind; and then the music began again—
something distant, and sad, and yearning,
like the cry of a soul seeking for light in
the dark, for comfort in despair. Nan,
in her solitary pew, bowed her head and
covered her face with her hands. This
music was less picturesque, perhaps, than
that she had heard in the cathedral at
Lucerne, but it had more of a human cry
in it; it was an appeal for guidance—for
light—for light in the darkness of the
world. The tears were running down

Nan's face. And then there came into a neighbouring pew a woman dressed in a peculiar costume, all in black; and she, too, knelt down, and covered her face with her hands. And Nan would fain have gone to her and said—

'Oh, sister, take me with you and teach me. You have chosen your path in the world—the path of charity and good-will and peace; let me help you; let me give myself to the poor and the sick. There must be something somewhere for me to do in the world. Take me into your sisterhood; I am not afraid of hardship; let me be of some little use to those who are wretched and weary in heart.'

By and by that lady in black rose, went into the open space fronting the altar, knelt one knee slightly, and then left. Presently Nan followed her, her head bent down somewhat, and her heart not very light.

Just as she was leaving the interior of the church, some one stepped out of the vestry, followed her for a second, and then addressed her. She turned and recognised Mr. Jacomb. He had not been officiating; he was in ordinary clerical costume; and there was something in the primness of that costume that suited his appearance. For he was a singularly clean-looking man; his face smooth shaven; his complexion of the fairest white and pink; his hair yellow almost to whiteness; his eyes gray, clear, and kindly. For the rest, he was about six-and-thirty; of stoutish build; and he generally wore a pleasant and complacent smile, as if the world had treated him kindly, despite his experiences in that poor parish in the south-east of London, and as if, whatever might happen to him, anxiety was not likely to put a premature end to his existence.

' Dear me,' said he, 'what a coincidence! I saw your sister Madge about twenty minutes ago. She seemed very happy about something or other.'

' Mr. Jacomb,' said Nan, ' do you know the lady who left a minute ago?'

' No,' said he, wondering a little at the earnestness—or rather the absentness—of her manner. ' I only caught a glimpse of her. She belongs to one of the visiting sisterhoods.'

Nan was silent for a second or two.

' You came to the wedding, of course?' continued Mr. Jacomb, cheerfully. ' A capital match, that, for young De la Poer. She will have £18,000 a year when her mother dies; and she is pretty too. She puts a little side on, perhaps, when she's talking to strangers; but that's nothing. His brother was at Oxford when I was there, I remember—an awfully fast fellow; but they say all the sons of clergymen are; the other swing of the pendulum, you know. There's a medium in all things; and if one generation gives itself over too much to piety, the next goes as far the other way. I suppose it's human nature.'

This air of agreeable levity—this odour of worldliness (which was in great measure assumed)—did not seem to accord well with Nan's present mood. She was disturbed—uncertain—yearning for something she knew not what—and the echoes of that strange cry in the music were still in her soul. Mr. Jacomb's airs of being a man of the world—of being a clergyman

who scorned to attach any esoteric mystery
to his cloth, or to expect to be treated with
a particular reverence—might put him on
easy terms of friendship with Nan's sisters;
but they only made Nan regretful, and
sometimes even impatient. Did he imagine the assumption of flippancy made
him appear younger than he really was?
In any case it was bad policy so far as
Nan was concerned. Nan was a born
worshipper. She was bound to believe in
something or somebody. And the story
she had heard of the Rev. Charles Jacomb's
assiduous, earnest, uncomplaining labour
in that big parish had at the very outset
won for him her great regard. He did
not understand how he was destroying
her childlike faith in him by his saturnine
little jokes.

'Mr. Jacomb,' said Nan, timidly, 'I

should be so greatly obliged to you if you could find out something more for me about those sisterhoods. They must do a great deal of good. And their dress is such a protection; they can go anywhere without fear of rudeness or insult. I suppose it is not a difficult thing to get admission——'

He was staring at her in amazement.

' But not for you—not for you!' he cried. ' Why, it is preposterous for you to think of such a thing. There are plenty who have nothing else in the world to look forward to. You have all your life before you yet. My dear Miss Anne, you must not indulge in day-dreams. Look at your sister Madge. Oh, by-the-way, she said something about your mamma having sent me a note this morning, asking me to dine with you on Friday evening; and then remembering, after the note was posted, that on that evening you had taken a box for the pantomime. Well, there needs be no trouble about that, if I may join your party to go there also.'

Nan said nothing; but perhaps there was the slightest trace of surprise, or interrogation, in her look. Immediately he said—

'Oh, I very much approve of panto-mimes, from a professional point of view—I do, really. You see, the imagination of most people is very dull—it wants a stimu-lus—and I am perfectly certain, if the truth were known, that the great majority of people in this country have derived their pictorial notions of heaven from the trans-formation-scenes in pantomimes. I am certain of it. John Martin's pictures—the only other alternative—are not striking enough. So, on the whole, I very much approve of pantomimes; and I shall be very glad to go with you on Friday, if I may.'

Nan made some excuse, shook hands with him, and went. She walked home hurriedly, she knew not why; it almost seemed as though she wanted to leave something well behind her. And she was very kind to her sisters for the remainder of that day; but somewhat grave.

Meanwhile, Madge's letter to her married sister in London had been sent. And the first answer to it was contained in a postscript to a letter addressed by Mary Beresford to her mother. This was the postscript :—

'*What is this nonsense Madge writes to me about herself and Holford King? Has Captain King got it into his head that he would like to marry his deceased wife's sister?'*

Lady Beresford threw the letter aside with a sigh, wishing people would not write in conundrums.

CHAPTER XVII.

THE ACCEPTED SUITOR.

'Oh, Nan, here is the cab. What shall I say to him? What am I to say to him?'

'I think you ought to know yourself, dear,' said Nan, gently, and then she slipped away from the room, leaving Madge alone and standing at the window.

But after all it was not so serious a matter. Some one came into the room, and Madge turned.

'May I call you Madge?' said he, holding both her hands.

She answered, with her eyes cast
down—

'I suppose I must call you Frank.'

That was all, for at the same moment
Mr. Tom was heard calling to his mother
and sisters that Captain King had arrived ;
and directly after, Lady Beresford and
Edith entered the room, followed by Mr.
Tom, who was declaring that they must
have dinner put forward to six o'clock, if
they were all to go to the pantomime.

There was a little embarrassment—not
much.   Frank King kept looking towards
the door.   He wondered why Nan had
not come with the others.   He was curious to see how much she had changed.
Perhaps he should not even recognise her ?
Without scarcely knowing why, he was
hoping she might not be quite like the
Nan of former days.

Mr. Tom consulted his watch again.

'Shall I ring and tell them to hurry on dinner, mother?'

'We cannot alter the dinner hour now,' Lady Beresford said, plaintively. 'It has already been altered once. Both Mr. Roberts and Mr. Jacomb promised to come at half-past six, so that you might all go to the pantomime together in good time.'

'What?' cried Mr. Tom. 'Jacomb? Did you say Jacomb, mother?'

'I said Mr. Roberts and Mr. Jacomb,' said his mother.

'And what the etcetera is he doing in that gallery!' exclaimed Mr. Tom. 'Well, I guess we shall have a high old time of it at dinner. Soda-water and incense. But there's one thing they always agree about. Get them on to port-wine vintages, and they run together like a brace of greyhounds.'

Here Captain King begged to be excused, as there was but little time for him to go along to his hotel and get dressed for this early dinner. When—being accompanied to the door by Mr. Tom himself—he had left, Madge said—

'How do you like him, mamma? Are you pleased with him?'

'He has not spoken to me yet, you know,' said the mother, wearily; she had had to go through several such scenes, and they worried her.

'Oh, but it's all arranged,' Madge said, cheerfully. 'He won't bother you about a solemn interview. It's all arranged. How did you think he looked, Edith? I do hope he won't lose that brown colour by not going back to sea; it suits him; I don't like pastey-faced men. Now, Mr. Jacomb isn't pastey-faced, although he is a clergyman. By-the-way, what has become of Nan?'

Nan had been quite forgotten. Perhaps she was dressing early, or looking after the dinner-table; at all events, it was time for the other sisters to go and get ready also.

Punctual to the moment, Captain King arrived at the door, and entered, and went upstairs. He was not a little excited. Now he would see Nan—and not only her, but also this clergyman, whom he was also curious to see. At such a moment—arriving as Madge's accepted suitor—it was not Nan that he ought to have been thinking about. But it was Nan whom his first quick glance round the drawing-room sought out; and instantly he knew she was not there.

Everybody else was, however. Mr.

Roberts, with his conspicuous red opal and diamonds, was standing on the hearth-rug with his back to the fire, talking to Lady Beresford, who was cushioned up in an easy-chair. Mr. Jacomb was enter-taining the two sisters, Edith and Madge, who were laughing considerably. Mr. Tom was walking about with his hands in his pockets, ferocious, for dinner was already eighteen seconds late.

Frank King had not much time to study the looks or manners of this clergy-man, to whom he was briefly introduced; for already his attention, which was at the moment exceedingly acute, was drawn to the opening of the door. It was Nan who slipped in, quietly. Apparently she had seen the others before; for when she caught sight of him, she at once ad-vanced towards him, with a grave, quiet smile on her face, and an outstretched hand.

'Oh, how do you do, Captain King?' she said, in the most friendly way, and without the least trace of embarrassment.

Of course she looked at his eyes as she said so. Perhaps she did not notice the strange, startled look that had dwelt there for an instant as he regarded her—a look as if he had seen some one whom he had not expected to see—some one whom he almost feared to see. He could not speak, indeed. For the moment he had really lost command of himself, and seemed bewildered. Then he stammered—

'How do you do, Miss Anne? I am glad to see you looking so well. You— you have not altered much—anything— during these last three or four years.'

'Oh, Nan has altered a great deal I

can tell you,' said Mr. Tom; 'and for the
better.   She isn't half as saucy as she
used to be.'

But Nan had turned to her mother, to
say privately—

'They are quite ready, mamma.   The
shades just came in time; and the candles
are all lit now.'

Then she turned to Captain King
again.   If she was acting non-embarrass-
ment, she was acting very well.   The
clear, friendly, gray-blue eyes regarded
him with frankness; there was no touch
of tell-tale colour in the fair, piquant,
freckled face; she smiled, as if to one in
whom she had perfect confidence.

'It is so kind of you,' she said, 'to
have let my brother pay you a visit to
Kingscourt; I am afraid he must be dull
here sometimes.   And he says he enjoyed

it immensely, and that every one was so
kind to him. I hope he didn't disgrace
himself—I mean in the shooting; you see
he has not had a great deal of practice.'

'Oh, he shot very well,' said Captain
Frank King, somewhat hurriedly. 'Oh
yes, very well. I should call him a very
good shot. I am glad he liked his visit.'
But Frank King was not looking into
Nan's eyes as he spoke.

Then some one at the door said,
'Dinner is served, your Ladyship;' and the
company arranged themselves according
to order, and went downstairs. It fell to
Captain King's lot to go down last, with
Lady Beresford; but when they reached the
dining-table he found that his neighbour
was to be Madge, and he was glad of that.

Nan was opposite to him; he had discovered that at the first glance, and there-

after he rather avoided looking that way. He endeavoured to entertain Lady Beresford, and occasionally spoke a little to Madge ; but he was somewhat preoccupied on the whole ; and very frequently he might have been caught regarding the clergyman-guest with an earnest scrutiny. Mr. Jacomb, to do him justice, was making himself the friend of everybody. He could talk well and pleasantly ; he had a number of little jokes and stories ; and he was making himself generally agreeable. The efflorescent Roberts was anxious to know —as anxious, that is, as a very devoted regard for his *menu* would permit—the precise position held by a certain High Churchman who was being harried and worried by the law courts at this time ; but Mr. Jacomb, with great prudence, would have nothing to say on such subjects. He laughed the whole matter off. He preferred to tell anecdotes about his Oxford days ; and gave you to understand that these were not far removed from the present time. You might have guessed that he and his companions were the least little bit wild. The names of highly respectable dignitaries in the Church were associated with stories of scrapes that were quite alarming, and with sayings that just bordered here and there on the irreverent. But then, to a clergyman much is permitted ; for it is his business to know where the line should be drawn ; other people might not feel quite so safe.

All this time Captain Frank King was intently regarding Mr. Jacomb ; and Nan saw it. The smile died away from her face. She grew self-absorbed; she scarcely lifted her eyes.

'Nan, what's the matter with you?' said her brother Tom to her, privately. 'You're not going to cry, are you?'

She looked up with her frank, clear eyes, and said—

'I was trying to remember some lines near the beginning of *Faust*. They are about a clergyman and a comedian.'

This was beyond Mr. Tom; and so he said nothing. But what Nan had meant had been uttered in a moment of bitterness, and was entirely unjust. Mr. Jacomb was not failing in any proper respect for his sacred calling. But he was among some young people; he hoped they would not think his costume coercive; he wished to let them know that his youth also had only been the other day, as it were, and that he appreciated a joke as well as any one. If his speech at the moment was

frivolous—and, indeed, intentionally frivolous—his life had not been frivolous. He
had never intrigued or cajoled for prefer-
ment, but had done the work that lay
nearest him. At Oxford he had toadied
no one. And his 'record,' as the Ameri-
cans say, in that parish in the south-east of
London, was unblemished and even noble.

But he made a hash of it that evening,
somehow. Nan Beresford grew more and
more depressed and disheartened—almost
ashamed. If Frank King had not been
there, perhaps she would have cared less ;
but she knew—without daring to look—
that Frank King was regarding and listening with an earnest and cruel scrutiny.

When the time came for their starting
for the theatre, Nan disappeared. Tom
began to make a noise, and then the message came that, Please sir, Miss Anne had a

headache, and might she be excused? Tom made a further noise, and declared that the whole thing must be put off. Go to see a pantomime without Nan he would not. Then a further message came from Miss Anne, saying that she would be greatly distressed if they did not go; and so, after no end of growling and grumbling, Mr. Tom put his party into two cabs and took them off. Nan heard the roll of the wheels lessen and cease.

It was about half-past eleven that night that someone noisily entered Nan's room, and lit the gas. Nan opening her eyes— for she was in bed and asleep—beheld a figure there, all white with snow.

'Oh, Nan,' said this new-comer, in great excitement, ' I must tell you all about it. There has been such fun. Never such a gale known on the south coast——'

'Child!' said the now thoroughly awakened sister, 'go at once and take off your things. You will be wet through!'

'Oh, this is nothing,' said Madge, whose pink cheeks showed what she had faced. 'I left a whole avalanche in the hall. The streets are a foot deep already. Not a cab to be got. We had to fight our way from the theatre arm in arm; the wind and snow were like to lift us off our feet altogether. Frank said it reminded him of Canada. All the gentlemen are below; Tom would have them come in to get them some mulled claret.'

Madge's ejaculatory sentences came to an end simply for want of breath. She was all panting.

'Such a laughing there was! Frank and I ran full tilt against a gentleman who was coming full sail before the wind.

" Hard-a-port!" Frank cried. There was an awful smash. My hat blew off; and we hid in a doorway till Frank got it back again.'

At Nan's earnest entreaties, her younger sister at last consented to take off her outer garments and robe herself in some of Nan's —meantime shaking a good deal of snow on to the carpet. Then she came and sat down.

' I must tell you all about it, dear Nan,' she said, ' for I am so happy ; and it has been such a delightful evening. You can't imagine what a splendid companion Frank is—taking everything free and easy, and always in such a good humour. Well, we went to the theatre ; and of course Edith wanted to show herself off, so I had the corner of the box with the curtains, and Frank sat next me, of course—it was

" Cinderella" — beautiful ! — I never saw such brilliant costumes ; and even Edith was delighted with the way they sang the music. Mind, we didn't know that by this time the storm had begun. It was all like fairyland. But am I tiring you, Nan ?' said Madge with a sudden compunction. ' Would you rather go to sleep again ?'

' Oh no, dear.'

' Is your headache any better ?'

' A great deal.'

' Shall I get you some eau-de-cologne ?'

' Oh no.'

' Does it sound strange to you that I should call him Frank ? It did to me at first. But of course it had to be done ; so I had to get over it.'

'You don't seem to have had much difficulty,' said Nan, with an odd kind of smile.

'Well,' Madge confessed, 'he isn't like other men. There's no pretence about him. He makes friends with you at once. And you can't be very formal with any one who is lugging you through the snow.'

'No, of course not,' said Nan gravely. 'I was not saying there could be anything wrong in calling him Frank.'

'Well, the pantomime; did I tell you how good it was? Mr. Roberts says he never saw such beautifully-designed dresses in London; and the music was lovely— oh! if you had heard Cinderella, how she sang, you would have fallen in love with her, Nan. We all did. Then we had ices. There's a song which Cinderella sings Frank promised to get for me; but I can't sing. All I'm good for is to show off Edith.'

'You ought to practise more, dear.'

'But it's no good once you are married.
You always drop it. If I have any time
I'll take to painting. You see you have
no idea, in a house like this, the amount
of trouble there is in keeping up a place
like Kingscourt.'

'But you know, Madge, Mrs. Holford
King is there.'

'She can't be there always; she's very
well up in years,' said the practical Madge.
'And you know the whole estate is now
definitely settled on Frank—though there
are some heavy mortgages. We shan't be
able to entertain much for the first few
years, I dare say—but we shall always be
glad to have you, Nan.'

Nan did not say anything; she turned
her face away a little bit.

'Nan,' said her sister, presently, 'didn't
Mary and Edith have a notion that Captain

King was at one time rather fond of you?'

Nan's face flushed hastily.

'They—they—imagined something of that kind, I believe.'

'But was it true?'

Nan raised herself up, and took her sister's hand in her two hands.

'You see, dear,' she said, gently, and with her eyes cast down, 'young men— I mean very young men—have often passing fancies that don't mean very much. Later on they make their serious choice.'

'But,' said Madge, persistently, 'but I suppose he never really asked you to be his wife?'

'His wife!' said Nan, with well-simulated surprise. 'Recollect, Madge, I was just over seventeen. You don't promise

to be anybody's wife at an age like that;
you are only a child then.'

'I am only eighteen,' said Madge.

'But there is a great difference. And
recollect that Captain King is now older,
and knows better what his wishes are,
and what way his happiness lies. You
ought to be very proud, Madge; and you
should try to make him proud of you also.'

'Oh, I will, Nan; I will really. I wish
you would teach me a lot of things.'

'What things?'

'Oh, you know. All the sort of stuff
that you know. Tidal waves and things.'

'But Captain King won't have anything
more to do with tidal waves.'

'Then we'll go round the shops to-
morrow, Nan; and you'll tell me about
Chippendale furniture and blue china.'

'Don't you think there will be enough

of that at Kingscourt; and just such things as you couldn't get to buy in any shops ?'

' Then what am I to do, Nan ?'

' You can try to be a good wife, dear ; and that's better than anything.'

Madge rose.

' I'll let you off, Nan. But I do feel terribly selfish. I haven't said a single word about you——'

' Oh, but I don't want anything said about me,' said Nan, almost in alarm.

' Well, you know, Nan, everybody says this : that a clergyman's wife has more opportunities of doing good than any other women ; for, you see, they are in the middle of it all, and they can interfere as no one else can, and it is expected of them, and the poor people don't object to them as they might to others.'

' Oh, I think that is quite true,' said

Nan, thoughtfully—perhaps with a slight sigh. 'Yes, I have often thought of that.'

'And you know, dear, that was what Providence meant you to be,' said Madge, with a friendly smile. 'That is just what you were made for—to be kind to other people. Good-night, old Mother Nan!'

'Good-night, dear.'

They kissed each other; and Madge turned off the gas and left. Presently, however, Madge returned, opened the door, and came in on tiptoe.

'Nan, you are not asleep yet?'

'Of course not.'

'I wanted to ask you, Nan; do you think he would like me to work a pair of slippers for him?'

'No doubt he would,' was the quiet answer.

'For I was thinking it would be so

nice if you would come with me to-morrow and help me to choose the materials ; and then, you see, Nan, you might sketch me some design, out of your own head, for you are so clever at those things, and that would be better than a shop pattern. And then,' added Madge, ' I should tell him it was your design.'

Nan paused for a second.

' I will do whatever you want, Madge —but you must not say that I made the design for you. It won't be worth much at the best. I would rather have nothing said about it, dear.'

' Very well, Nan ; that's just like you.'

CHAPTER XVIII.

A WHITE WORLD.

NEXT morning it still snowed and blew hard; no one could go out; it was clearly a day to be devoted to indoor amusements. And then Frank King, despite the state of the streets and the absence of cabs, made his way along, and was eagerly welcomed. As Mr. Tom's companion he was to spend the whole day there. Billiards, music, lunch, painting — they would pass the time somehow. And meanwhile the gusts of wind rattled the windows; and the whirling snow blurred out the sea; and Mr. Tom kept on big fires.

Nan remained in her own room. When Madge went up to bring her down she found her reading Thomas à Kempis.

'Frank has asked twice where you were,' Madge remonstrated.

'But that is not a command,' said Nan, with a smile. 'I should have thought, judging by the sound, that you were being very well amused below.'

Madge went away, and in about an hour after came back. She found that her sister had put away *De Imitatione Christi*, and was at her desk.

'Writing! To whom?'

'To the Editor of the *Times*,' said Nan, laughing at her sister's instantaneous dismay.

'The *Times*? Are you going to turn a blue-stocking, Nan?'

'Oh no; it's only about blankets. You can read the letter; do you think he will print it?'

This was the letter which Madge read, and which was written in a sort of handwriting that some editors would be glad to see oftener :—

'Dear Sir,—The Government interfere to punish a milkman who adulterates milk with water; and I wish to put the question in your columns why they should not also punish the manufacturers who dress blankets with arsenic? Surely it is a matter of equal importance. Poor people can get along without milk, unless there are very small children in the house; but when they have insufficient food, and insufficient fire, and scant clothes, and perhaps also a leaky roof, a good warm pair of blankets is almost a necessity. You cannot imagine what a compensation it is, especially in weather like the present; but how are the charitably disposed to take such a gift to a poor household when it may become the instrument of death or serious illness? Dear Sir, I hope you will call upon the Government to put down this wicked practice; and I am, yours respectfully,   AN ENGLISH GIRL.'

'Oh, that's all right,' said Madge, who had feared that her sister had taken to literature; 'that's quite the right thing for you. Of course, a clergyman's wife must know all about blankets, and soup-kitchens, and things.'

Nan flushed a little, and said quickly and with an embarrassed smile—

'I thought of putting in something about his "eloquent pen" or his "generous advocacy," but I suppose he gets a great deal of that kind of flattery, and isn't to be taken in. I think I will leave it as it is. It is really most shameful that such things should be allowed.'

'When are you coming down to see Frank?'

'By and by, dear. I am going now to get mamma her egg and port wine.'

'I know Frank wants to see you.'

'Oh, indeed,' she said, quietly, as she folded up the letter.

That memorable snowstorm raged all day; the shops fronting the sea were shut; the whole place looked like some vast, deserted, white City of the Dead. But towards evening the squalls moderated; that fine, penetrating, crystalline snow ceased to come in whirls and gusts; and people began to get about, the black figures making their way over or through the heavy drifts, or striking for such places as the force of the wind had driven bare. Here and there shovels were in requisition to open a pathway; it was clearly thought that the gale was over; the Beresfords and their guest began to speak of an excursion next day to Stanmer Park, lest peradventure it might be possible to have a lane or two swept on the ice for a little skating.

The next morning proved to be brilliantly beautiful; and they were all up and away betimes on their somewhat hopeless quest. All, that is to say, except Nan: for she had sundry pensioners to look after, who were likely to have fared ill during the inclement weather. Nan put on her thickest boots and her ulster, and went out into the world of snow. The skies were blue and clear; the air was fresh and keen; it was a relief to be out after that monotonous confinement in the house.

Nan went her rounds, and wished she was a millionaire, for the fine snow had penetrated everywhere, and there was great distress. Perhaps she was really trying to imagine herself a clergyman's wife; at all events, when she had grown tired, and perhaps a little heart-sick, it was no wonder that she should think of going into that church, which was always open, for a little rest, and solace, and soothing quiet.

This was what she honestly meant to do—and, moreover, it was with no expectation of meeting Mr. Jacomb there, for it was almost certain that he also would be off on a round of visitations. She had a craving for quiet; perhaps some slow, grateful music would be filling the air;

there would be silence in the vast, hushed place.

Well, it was by the merest accident that her eyes happened to light on a vessel that was scudding up channel under double-reefed topsails, and she stood for a minute to watch it. Then she, also inadvertently, perceived that the coastguardsman over the way had come out of his little box, and was similarly watching the vessel — through his telescope. Nan hesitated for a second. The snow was deep, though a kind of path had been trodden a few yards farther along. Then she walked quickly on till she came to that path, crossed, went back to the coastguardsman, and addressed him, with a roseate glow on her cheek.

'Oh, I beg your pardon—but—but—I suppose you know Singing Sal?'

'Yes, Miss,' said the little Celtic-looking man with the brown beard. He was evidently surprised.

'Do you know where she is? I hope she wasn't in the storm yesterday? She hasn't been along this way lately?'

'No, Miss; not that I knows of.'

'Thank you, I am very much obliged.'

'Wait a minute, Miss—Wednesday—yes, it was last night, I believe, as Sal was to sing at a concert at Updene. Yes, it was. Some o' my mates at Cuckmere got leave to go.'

'Updene farm?'

'Yes, Miss,' said the wiry little sailor with a grin. 'That's promotion for Sal—to sing at a concert.'

'I don't see why she should not sing at a concert,' said Nan, regarding him with her clear gray eyes, so that the grin instantly vanished from his face. 'I've heard much worse singing at many a concert. Then, if she was at Updene last night, she would most likely come along here to-day.'

'I don't know, Miss,' said the man, who knew much less about Singing Sal's ways than did Miss Anne Beresford. 'Mayhap the concert didn't come off, along of the snow.'

Nan again thanked him, and continued on her way—eastward. She was thinking. Somehow she had quite forgotten about the church. The air around her was wonderfully keen and exhilarating; the skies overhead were intensely blue; out there on the downs the soft, white snow would be beautiful. Nan walked on at a brisker pace, and her spirits rose. The sunlight seemed to get into her veins. And then

her footing required a great deal of attention, and she had plenty of active exercise;
for though here and there the force of the
wind had left the roads almost bare, else-
where the snow had formed long drifts of
three to five feet in depth, and these had
either to be got round or plunged through.
Then, up Kemp-Town way, where there
is less traffic, her difficulties increased.
The keen air seemed to make her easily
breathless. But at all events she felt com-
fortably warm, and the sun felt hot on her
cheek.

She had at length persuaded herself
that she was anxious about Singing Sal's
safety. Many people must have perished
in that snowstorm—caught unawares on
the lonely downs. At all events, she could
ask at one or two of the coastguard stations
if anything had been heard of Sal. It was

just possible she might meet her, if the entertainment at Updene farm had come off.

At Black Rock station they had heard nothing; but she went on all the same. For now this was a wonderful and beautiful landscape all around her, up on these high cliffs; and the novelty of it delighted her, though the bewildering white somewhat dazzled her eyes. Towards the edge of the cliffs, where the wind had swept across, there was generally not more than an inch or two of snow—hard and crisp, with traceries of birds' feet on it, like long strings of lace; but a few yards on her left the snow had got banked up in the most peculiar drifts, resembling in a curious manner the higher ranges of the Alps. Sometimes, however, the snow became deep here also; so that she had to betake herself to the

road, where the farmers' men around had
already cut a way through the deeper
stoppages ; and there she found herself
going along a white gallery—yellow-white
on the left, where the sunlight fell on the
snow, but an intense blue on the right,
where the crystalline snow, in shadow,
reflected the blue of the sky overhead.
And still she ploughed on her way, with
all her pulses tingling with life and gladness; for this wonder of yellow whiteness
and blue whiteness, and the sunlight, and
the keen air, all lent themselves to a kind
of fascination ; and she scarcely perceived
that her usual landmarks were gone : it
was enough for her to keep walking,
stumbling, sinking, avoiding the deeper
drifts, and farther and farther losing herself in the solitariness of this white, hushed
world

Then, far away, and showing very black against the white, she perceived the figure of a woman, and instantly jumped to the conclusion that that must be Singing Sal. But what was Sal—if it were she—about? That dark figure was wildly swaying one arm like an orator declaiming to an excited assemblage. Had the dramatic stimulus of the previous night's entertainment—Nan asked herself—got into the woman's brain? Was she reciting poetry to that extravagant gesturing? Nan walked more slowly now, and took breath; while the woman, whoever she was, evidently was coming along at a swinging pace.

No; that was no dramatic gesture. It was too monotonous. It looked more as if she were sowing—to imperceptible furrows. Nan's eyes were very long-sighted, but this thing puzzled her altogether. She now certainly looked like a farmer's man scattering seed-corn.

Singing Sal saw and recognised her young-lady friend at some distance, and seemed to moderate her gestures, though these did not quite cease. When she came up, Nan said to her:

' What are you doing?'

'Well, Miss,' she said, with a bright smile—her face was quite red with the cold air, and her hair not so smooth as she generally kept it—'my arm does ache, to tell the truth. And my barley's nearly done. I have tried to scatter it wide, so as the finches and larks may have a chance, even when the jackdaws and rooks are at it.'

' Are you scattering food for the birds, then?'

' They're starved out in this weather,

Miss; and then the boys come out wi'
their guns; and the dicky-laggers are
after them too——'

'The what?'

'The bird-catchers, Miss. If I was a
farmer now, I'd take a horsewhip, I would,
and I'd send those gentry double quick
back to Whitechapel. And the gentle-
folks, Miss, it isn't right of them to encourage the trapping of larks when there's
plenty of other food to be got. Well, my
three-penn'orth o' barley that I bought in
Newhaven is near done now.'

She looked into the little wallet that
she had twisted round in front of her.

'Oh, if you don't mind,' said Nan,
eagerly, 'I will give you a shilling—or
two or three shillings — to get some
more.'

'You could do better than that, Miss,'

said Sal. 'Maybe you know some one that lives in Lewes Crescent?'

'Yes, I do.'

'Well, ye see, Miss, there's such a lot o' birds as won't eat grain at all; and if you was to get the key of the garden in Lewes Crescent, and get a man to sweep the snow off a bit of the grass, and your friends might throw down some mutton bones and scraps from the kitchen, and the birds from far and near would find it out—being easily seen, as it might be. Half the thrushes and blackbirds along this countryside 'll be dead before this snow gives out.'

'Oh, I will go back at once and do that,' said Nan, readily.

'Look how they've been running about all the morning,' said this fresh-coloured, dark-eyed woman, regarding the traceries on the snow at her feet. 'Most of them larks—you can see the spur. And that's a rook with his big heavy claws. And there's a hare, Miss—I should say he was trotting as light as could be—and there's nothing uglier than a trotting hare—he's like a race-horse walking—all stiff and jolting, because of the high aunches— haunches, Miss. They're all bewildered- like, birds and beasts the same. I saw the pad of a fox close by Rottingdean; he must have come a long way to try for a poultry-yard. And, what's rarer, I saw a covey of partridges, Miss, settle down on the sea as I was coming along by Salt- dean Gap. They was tired out, poor things, and not driven before the wind either, but fighting against it, and going out to sea blind-like; and then I saw them sink down on to the water, and then the waves knocked them about anyway. I hear there was a wonderful sight of brent geese up by Berling Gap yesterday—but I'm keeping you standing in the cold, Miss——'

'I will walk back with you,' said Nan, turning.

'No, Miss. No, thank you, Miss,' said Sal, sturdily.

'But only as far as Lewes Crescent,' said Nan, with a gentle laugh. 'You know I am going to stop there for the mutton bones. I want to know what has happened to you since the last time I saw you—that's a good while ago now.'

'Two things, Miss, has happened that I'm proud of,' said Sal, as the two set out to face the brisk westerly wind. 'I was taking a turn through Surrey, and when I was at ——, they told me that a great poet lived close by there—Mr. ——'

'Of course every one knows Mr. ——,' said Nan.

'I didn't,' said Sal, rather shamefacedly. 'You see, Miss, the two I showed you are enough company for me; and I haven't got money to buy books wi'. Well, I was passing near the old gentleman's house, and he came out, and he spoke to me as we went along the road. He said he had seen me reading the afternoon before, on the common; and he began to speak about poetry; and then he asked me if I had read any of Mr. ——'s, without saying he was himself. I was sorry to say no, Miss, for he was such a kind old gentleman; but he said he would send me them; and most like they're waiting for me now at Goring, where I gave him an address. Lor, the questions he asked me!—about Shakespeare and Burns—you know, Miss, I had them in my bag; and then about myself. I shouldn't wonder if he wrote a poem about me.'

'Well, that's modest,' said Nan, with another quiet laugh.

Sal did not at all like that gentle reproof.

'It isn't my pride, Miss; it's what he said to me that I go by,' she retorted. 'I didn't ask him.'

'If he does, all England will hear about you then,' said Nan. 'And now, what was the other thing?'

Sal again grew shamefaced a little. She opened the inner side of her wallet, took out a soiled, weather-beaten copy of the *Globe* Shakespeare, and from it extracted a letter.

'Perhaps you would like to read it yourself, Miss,' she suggested.

Nan took it, and had little difficulty in deciphering its contents, though the lan-

guage was occasionally a trifle hyperboli-
cal. It contained nothing less than an offer
of marriage addressed to Sal by a sailor
in one of Her Majesty's ironclads, who
said that he was tired of the sea, and that,
if Sal would give up her wandering life, so
would he, and he would retire into the
coastguard. He pointed out the sacrifices
he was ready to make for her; for it appeared that he was a petty officer. No
matter; he was willing to become simple
A.B. again; for he had his 'feelin's;' and
if so be as she would become his wife, then
they would have a good weather-proof
cottage, a bit of garden, and three-and-
fourpence a day. It was a most business-
like, sensible offer.

'And I'm sure I could do something
for him,' Nan eagerly said. 'I think I
could get him promotion. The Senior

Naval Lord of the Admiralty is a friend of mine. And wouldn't it be better for you?'

'No, Miss,' said Sal, with an odd kind of smile. 'I was glad to get the letter, for it shows I'm respected. But I'm not going to be caged yet. I never saw or heard of the man I would marry—except it might have been Robbie Burns, if he was still alive. Sometimes when I've been reading a bit, coming along the downs all by myself like, I've seen somebody in the distance; and I've said to myself, "Well, now, if that was only to turn out to be that black-a-vised Ayrshire ploughman, it would be all over with me; it would be 'Whistle and I'll come to ye, my lad.'" And then some shambling fellow of a labourer has come along, straw-haired, bent-backed, twisted-kneed, and scarcely enough spirit

in him to say, " Marnin t' ye—good marnin
t' ye, wench !" '

'You are very independent,' said the
sage Nan. 'And that's all very well, as
long as your health lasts. But you might
become ill. You would want relatives and
friends, and a home. And in the coastguard houses you would have a very
comfortable home, and a garden to look
after; and your husband might get promotion.'

'If ever I marry,' said Sal, shaking her
head, 'it won't be one of the man-of-war's
men. They've just as little spirit or in-
dependence as the day labourers. They've
had it all crushed out of them by the hard
usage of the officers.'

'Oh, how can you say so !' said Nan,
warmly. 'The officers are English gentlemen. In former days there may have

been cruelty, but I am certain that exists
no longer. I know several officers : kinder-
hearted men don't exist. Why, there is a
captain in the navy——'

She stopped in great embarrassment.
But Singing Sal, not heeding, said, laconi-
cally—

'It ain't the captain, Miss. He's too
great a gentleman to interfere. It's the
first lieutenant, who can make the ship a
hell upon earth if he has a mind to. Ah!
Miss, it's little you know of the discipline
that goes on on board a man-o'-war.
There's no human being could stand it
who wasn't brought up to it. The merchantmen can't stand it, and won't stand
it ; that's where the officers find a difficulty
when the Reserves are called out. You
wouldn't find a man-o'-war's man marching
up to the First Lord of the Admiralty with

a lump of salt beef in his hand and asking him if it was fit to eat. And this Lord, Miss, being a civilian like, he never thought of having the man clapped in irons: "Throw it overboard," says he. "I will see that no more o' that kind of stuff is issued to her Majesty's fleet." That was the story I heard, Miss: the men were laughing about it at Beachy Head. And then, in the merchantmen Jack has a better chance, if he is a smart fellow——'

And so forth. They had once more got on to the subject of sailors and officers, regarded from their different points of view; and it was not until they had reached Brighton that the sight of Lewes Crescent reminded Nan that she had now to part from her companion and go in search of mutton bones for the thrushes and blackbirds.

CHAPTER XIX.

BREAKING DOWN.

Not only was she successful in this work of charity, but she must needs also institute a similar system of outdoor relief at her own end of the town; so that it was nearly dusk when she re-entered the house in Brunswick Terrace. She did not think of asking if there were any visitors; she went upstairs; perceived that the drawing-room door was an inch or two open, and was just about to enter when she heard voices. Inadvertently she paused.

It was Mr. Jacomb's voice. Then her mother said—

'I married happily myself, and I have never tried to influence my daughters——'

Nan shrank back, like a guilty thing. She had only listened to discover whether it was some one she knew who had called; but these few words of her mother's made her heart jump. She stole away noiselessly to her own room. She sat down, anxious and agitated, fearing she scarcely knew what.

She was not long left in suspense. Her mother came into the room and shut the door.

'I thought I heard you come in, Nan,' she said; 'and it's lucky you have, for Mr. Jacomb is here.'

'But I don't want to see Mr. Jacomb, mamma,' she said, breathlessly.

'He wants to see you,' her mother said, quietly; 'and I suppose you know what it is about.'

'I—I suppose so—yes, I can guess ——. Oh, mother, dear!' cried Nan, going and clinging to her mother. 'Do me this great kindness! I can't see him. I don't want to see him. Mother, you will go and speak to him for me!'

'Well, that is extraordinary,' said Lady Beresford, who, however, had far too great a respect for her nerves to become excited over this matter or anything else. 'That's a strange request. I have just told him I would not interfere. Of course I don't consider it a good match; you might do a great deal better from a worldly point of view. But you have always been peculiar, Nan. If you think it would be for your happiness to become a poor clergyman's wife, I will not oppose it. At the same time, I have always thought you might do better——'

'Oh, mother, don't you understand?' Nan broke in. 'It's to ask him to go away! I'm so sorry. If he had spoken before, I would have told him before——'

'You mean you refuse him, and I am to take the message,' said her mother, staring at her. 'That is all?'

The girl was silent.

'I must say, Nan, you have been acting very strangely. You have led us all to believe that you were going to marry him. Why did you let the man come about the house?'

'Don't speak like that to me, mother,' said Nan, with her under lip beginning to quiver. 'I—I tried to think of it. I knew he wanted me to be his wife; I thought it might be right; I thought I could do something that way; and—and I tried to persuade myself. But I can't marry him, mother—I can't—I don't wish to marry any one—I never will marry——'

'Don't talk nonsense, child!' said her mother, severely, for there was a sort of tendency towards excitement in the atmosphere. 'Let me understand clearly. I suppose you know your own mind. I am to go and tell this man definitely that you won't marry him?'

'Mother, don't put it in that harsh way. Tell him I am very sorry. Tell him I tried hard to think of it. Tell him I am sorry he has waited so long; but if he had asked sooner——'

'He would have had the same answer?'

The girl's face flushed red, and she said in a strange sort of way—

'Yes — perhaps so — I think it must have been the same answer at any time. Oh, I never, never could have brought myself to marry him! Mother, does it look cruel—does it look as if I had treated him badly?' she added, in the same anxious way.

'No, I would not say that,' answered her mother, calmly. 'A man must take his chance; and until he speaks he can't have an answer. I do not think Mr. Jacomb has any reason to complain—except, perhaps, that you don't go yourself and hear what he has to say——'

'Oh, mother, I couldn't do that. It would only be pain for both of us. And then I don't refuse him, you see, mother; that's something——'

Lady Beresford was uncertain. The truth was, she was not at all sorry to be

the bearer of this message—even at the
cost of a little trouble—for she did think
that her daughter ought to marry into a
better position in life. But she had just
been listening to what Mr. Jacomb had
to say for himself; and he had said a
good deal, not only about himself, but
about Nan, and her disposition, and what
would best secure her happiness, and so
forth. Lady Beresford had been just a
little bit impressed, and the question was
whether Nan ought not to be invited to a
fair consideration of the matter as repre-
sented by Mr. Jacomb himself.

'Well, Nan, if your mind is quite clear
about it——'

'Oh it is, mother,' she answered eagerly,
'quite—quite——'

That was an end. Her mother left
the room, slowly; Nan listened for her

footsteps until she heard her go into the
drawing - room and close the door. Her
first thought was to lock herself in, so
that there should be no appeal. Her next
was that it was excessively mean and
cruel of her to experience this wonderful
sense of relief, now that the die was irre-
vocably cast.

'If there was anything I could do for
him,' she was thinking—'anything—anything but that;' and then she listened
again to the stillness until she heard a bell
ring, and the drawing-room door open
again, and some one descend the stairs
into the hall. She felt guilty and sorry
at the same time. She wished she could
do something by way of compensation.
He would not think it was mere heartless-
ness? For indeed she had tried. And
would she not have done him a far

greater wrong if she had married him without being able to give him her whole heart ?

Nan went to the window; but it was too dark for her to see anything. She took it for granted he had gone away. She was glad, and ashamed of herself for being glad. She reproved herself. And then she had a vague sort of feeling that she would wear sackcloth and ashes—or try to be ten times kinder to everybody—or do something, anything, no matter what —to atone for this very unmistakable sense of gladness that seemed to pervade her whole being. She couldn't help it, because it was there; but she would do something by way of compensation. And the first thing she could think of was to go and brush the billiard-table with such thoroughness that Mr. Tom, when he came home should say he had never seen it in such good condition before.

That was a roaring party that somewhat later came in—all flushed faces and high spirits and delight; for they had walked all the way from Falmer over the downs, under the guidance of the Canadian experience of Frank King; and they had had wonderful adventures with the snowdrifts; and the night was beautiful—a crescent moon in the south, and high up in the south-east the gleaming belt of Orion. And Nan greatly entered into the joy of these adventurers, and wished to hear more of their futile efforts at skating; and was asking this one and the other about everything—until she found Mr. Tom's eyes fixed on her.

'Nan,' said he, with scrutiny and decision, 'you've been in the country to-day, walking.'

She admitted she had.

'And you had for your luncheon a bit of bread and an apple.'

'I generally take that as a precaution,' Nan said, simply.

'I thought so,' said Mr. Tom, with great satisfaction at his own shrewdness. 'I can tell in a minute. For you always come back looking highly pleased with yourself and inclined to be cheeky. I don't like the look of you when you're too set up. Your tongue gets too sharp. I'd advise you people to look out.'

Nan's conscience smote her. Was she so glad, then, that even outsiders saw it in her face? She became graver; and she vowed that she would be most reticent at dinner. Had she not promised to herself to try to be ten times kinder to everybody?

And she very soon, at dinner, had an opportunity of displaying her generosity. They were busy making havoc of the manner of a distinguished person who was much talked of at that time, and whom they had all chanced to meet. Now Nan ordinarily was very intolerant of affectation; but had she not promised to be ten times kinder to everybody? So she struck in in defence of this lady.

'But it is her nature to be affected,' said Nan. 'She is quite true to herself. That is her disposition. It wouldn't be natural for her to try not to be affected. She was born with that disposition. Look at the idiotic grimaces that infants make when they try to show they are pleased. And Mrs. —— wouldn't be herself at all if she wasn't affected. She might as well try to leave off her affectations as her clothes. She couldn't go about without any.'

'She goes about with precious little,' said Mr. Tom, who strongly disapproved of scanty ball-dresses. And then he added, 'But that's Nan all over. She's always for making the best of everything and everybody. It's always the best possible world with her.'

'And isn't that wise,' said Frank King, with a laugh, 'considering it's the only one we've got to live in at present?'

Nan was very bright and cheerful during this dinner, and Captain Frank King was most markedly attentive to her, and interested in her talking. When Nan began to speak, he seemed to consider that the whole table ought to listen; and his was the first look that approved, and the first laugh that followed. Then he discovered that she knew all sorts of out-of-the-way things that an ordinary young lady could by no possibility have been expected to know. It was more than ever clear to him that these solitary wanderings had taught her something. Where had she acquired all this familiarity, for example, with details about his own profession—or what had been his profession?

They went on to talk of the jeers of cabmen at each other, and how sharp some of them were. Then again they began to talk about other common sayings—the very origin of which had been forgotten ; and Frank King spoke of a taunt which was an infallible recipe for driving a bargee mad — ' *Who choked the boy with duff?*' — though nobody, not the bargees themselves, now knew anything whatever about the tragic incident that

must have happened sometime and somewhere.

'Yes,' said Nan at once, 'and there is
another like that that the collier-boats
can't stand. If you call out to a collier,
" *There's a rat in your chains*," he'd drive
his schooner ashore to get after you.'

'I suppose you have tried,' said her
mother, with calm dignity.

'I believe Nan spends most of her
time,' said the Beauty, 'in making mud-
pies with the boys in Shoreham Harbour.'

'Never you mind, Nan,' her brother
said, to encourage her. 'Next time we
go to Newhaven, you'll call out to the
colliers, " *There's a rat in your chains*," and
I'll stop behind a wall and watch them
beating you.'

All during that dinner Nan was both
amused and amusing, until a trifling little

incident occurred. She and Frank King on the other side of the table had almost monopolised the conversation, although quite unwittingly; and everybody seemed to regard this as a matter of course. Now it happened that Madge, who sat next her betrothed, made some slight remark to him. Perhaps he did not hear. At all events, he did not answer, but addressed Nan instead, with reference to something she had just been saying about lifeboats. Instantly, a hurt expression came over Madge's face, and as instantly Nan saw it. From that moment she grew more reserved. She avoided addressing herself directly to Captain Frank King. She devoted herself chiefly to her mother; and when, at the end of dinner, they adjourned in a body to the billiard-room (with the happy indifference of youth) she followed Lady Beresford up to the drawing-room and would herself make tea for her.

That night Madge came into Nan's room.

'Do you know, Nan,' she said, quite plainly, 'that whenever you are in the room Frank pays no attention to any one else?'

'I thought he was doing his best to amuse everybody at dinner,' Nan said—though she did not raise her eyes. 'He told some very good stories.'

'Yes, to you,' Madge insisted. Then she added, 'You know I like it. I hope he will always be good friends with all the family; for you see, Nan, it will be lonely for me at Kingscourt for a while, and of course I should like to have some-body from Brighton always in the house. And I know he admires you very much. He's always talking about your character, and your disposition, and your temperament, as if he had been studying you like a doctor. I suppose I've got no character, or he would talk about that sometimes. I don't understand it—that talking about something inside you, as if it was something separate from yourself; and calling it all kinds of sentiments and virtues, as if it was clockwork you couldn't see. I don't see anything like that in you, Nan—except that you are very kind, you know—but not so different from other people—as he seems to think.'

' It doesn't much matter what he thinks, does it ?' suggested Nan, gently.

' Oh no, of course not,' Madge said, promptly. ' He said I was a very good skater, considering the horrid condition of the ice. They have a large lake at Kingscourt.' Then after a pause, ' Nan, where did you learn all that about the lighthouses and the birds at night ?'

'Oh, that? I really don't know. What about it?—it is of no consequence.'

'But it interests people.'

'It ought not to interest you, or Captain King either. You will have to think of very different things at Kingscourt.'

'When you and Mr. Jacomb come to Kings——'

'Madge,' said Nan, quickly, 'you must not say anything like that. I do not mean to marry Mr. Jacomb, if that is what you mean.'

'No? Honour bright?'

'I shall not marry Mr. Jacomb; and I am not likely to marry any one,' she said, calmly. 'There are other things one can give one's life to, I suppose. It would be strange if there were not.'

Madge thought for a second or two.

'Oh, Nan,' she said cheerfully, 'it would be so nice to have an old-maid sister at Kingscourt. She could do such a lot of things, and be so nice and helpful, without the fuss and pretension of a married woman. It would be really delightful to have you at Kingscourt!'

'I hope, dear, you will be happy at Kingscourt,' said Nan, in a somewhat lower voice.

'I shall never be quite happy until you come to stay there,' said Madge, with decision.

'You will have plenty of occupation,' said Nan, absently. 'I have been thinking if a war broke out I should like to go as one of the nurses; and of course that wants training beforehand. There must be an institution of some kind, I suppose. Now, good-night, dear.'

'Good-night, Mother Nan. But we are not going to let you go away into wars. You are coming to Kingscourt. I know Frank will insist on it. And it would just be the very place for you; you see you would be in nobody's way; and you always were so fond of giving help. Oh, Nan,' her sister suddenly said, 'what is the matter? You are crying! What is it, Nan?'

Nan rose quickly.

'Crying? No—no—never mind, Madge—I am tired rather—there—good-night.'

She got her sister out of the room only in time. Her overstrained calmness had at length given way. She threw herself on the bed, and burst into a passion of weeping; and thus she lay far into the night, stifling her sobs so that no one should hear.

CHAPTER XX.

THE process of disenchantment is one of the saddest and one of the commonest things in life ; whether the cause of it be the golden youth who, apparently a very Bayard before marriage, after marriage gradually reveals himself to be hopelessly selfish, or develops a craving for brandy, or becomes merely brutal and ill-tempered; or whether it is the creature of all angelic gifts and graces who, after her marriage, destroys the romance of domestic life by her slatternly ways, or sinks into the condition of a confirmed sigher, or in time discovers to her husband that he has married a woman comprising in herself, to use the American phrase, nine distinct sorts of a born fool. These discoveries are common in life; but they generally follow marriage, which gives ample opportunities for study. Before marriage man and maid meet but at intervals; and then both are alike on their best behaviour. The slattern is no slattern now; she is always dainty and nice and neat; the golden youth is generous to a fault, and noble in all his ways; and if either or both should be somewhat foolish, or even downright stupid, the lack of wisdom is concealed by a tender smile or a soft touch of the hand. It is the dream-time of life; and it is not usual for one to awake until it is over.

But it was different with Frank King. The conditions in which he was placed were altogether peculiar. He had made two gigantic mistakes—the first in imagining that any two human beings could be alike : the second in imagining that, even if they were alike, he could transfer his affection from the one to the other—and he was now engaged in a hopeless and terrible struggle to convince himself that these were not mistakes. He would not see that Madge Beresford was very different from Nan. He was determined to find in her all he had hoped to find. He argued with himself that she was just like Nan, as Nan had been at her age. Madge was so kind, and good, and nice ; of course it would all come right in the end.

At the same time, he never wished to be alone with Madge, as is the habit of

lovers. Nor if he was suddenly interested
in anything did he naturally turn to her,
and call her attention. On the other
hand, the little social circle did not seem
complete when Nan, with her grave
humour, and her quiet smile, and her
gentle, kindly ways, was absent. When
she came into the room, then satisfaction
and rest were in the very air. If there
was a brighter green on the sea, where
a gleam of wintry sunshine struck the
roughened waters, whose eyes but Nan's
could see that properly ? It was she
whom he addressed on all occasions ;
perhaps unwittingly. It seemed so easy
to talk to Nan. For the rest, he shut
his eyes to other considerations. From
the strange fascination and delight that
house in Brunswick Terrace always had
for him, he knew he must be in love

with somebody there; and who could
that be but Madge Beresford, seeing that
he was engaged to her?

Unhappily for poor Madge, Frank
King was now called home by the old
people at Kingscourt; and for a time,
at least, all correspondence between him
and his betrothed would obviously have
to be by letter. Madge was in great
straits. A look, a smile, a touch of the
fingers may make up for lack of ideas;
but letter-writing peremptorily demands
them, of some kind or another. As usual,
Madge came to her elder sister.

'Oh, Nan, I do so hate letter-writing.
I promised to write every morning. I
don't know what in the world to say. It
is such a nuisance.'

Nan was silent; of late she had tried to
withdraw as much as possible from these

confidences of her sister's; but not very successfully. Madge clung to her. Lady Beresford would not be bothered. Edith was busy with her own affairs. But Nan —old Mother Nan—who had nothing to think of but other people, might as well begin and play the old maid at once, and give counsel in these distressing affairs.

' I wish you would tell me what to say,' continued Madge, quite coolly.

' I ? Oh, I cannot,' said Nan, almost shuddering, and turning away.

' But you know what interests him; for he's always talking to you,' persisted Madge, good-naturedly. 'Anybody but me would be jealous; but I'm not. The day before yesterday Mrs. —— went by; and I asked him to look at her hair, that every one is raving about; and he plainly told me your hair was the prettiest he had ever seen. Now, I don't call that polite. He might have said "except yours," if only for the look of the thing. But I don't mind—not a bit. I'm very glad he likes you, Nan——'

'Madge! Madge!'

It was almost a cry wrung from the heart. But in an instant she had controlled herself again. She turned to her sister, and said with great apparent calmness,

'Surely, dear, you ought to know what to write. These are things that cannot be advised about. Letters of that kind are secret——'

'Oh, I don't care about that. I think it is stupid,' said Madge at once. 'There is no use having any pretence about it. And I don't know in the world what to write about. Look,—I have begun about the Kenyons' invitation, and asked him whether he'd mind my going. I like those little dances better than the big balls——'

She held out the letter she had begun. But Nan would not even look at it.

'It isn't usual, is it, Madge,' she said, hurriedly, 'for a girl who is engaged to go out to a dance by herself?'

'But we are all going!'

'You know what I mean. It is a compliment you should pay him not to go.'

'Well,' said Madge somewhat defiantly, 'I don't know about that. One does as one is done by. And I don't think he'd care if I went and danced the whole night through—even with Jack Hanbury.'

'Oh, how can you say such a thing!' said her sister, staring at her; for this was a new development altogether.

But Madge was not to be put down.

'Oh, I am not such a fool. I can see well enough. There isn't much romance about the whole affair; and that's the short and the long of it. Of course it's a very good arrangement for both of us, I believe; and that's what they say now-a-days—marriages are " arranged." '

' I don't know what you mean, Madge ! You never spoke like that before.'

' Perhaps I was afraid of frightening you; for you have high and mighty notions of things, dear Nan, for all your mouse-like ways. But don't I see very well that he is marrying to please his parents; and to settle down and be the good boy of the family ? That's the meaning of the whole thing——'

' You don't mean to say, Madge,' said the elder sister, though she hesitated, and seemed to have to force herself to ask the question, 'You don't mean to say you think he does not—love you?'

At this Madge flushed up a little, and said—

'Oh, well, I suppose he does, in a kind of way, though he doesn't take much trouble about saying it. It isn't of much consequence; we shall have plenty of time afterwards. Mind, if only Jack Hanbury could get invited by the Kenyons, and I were to dance two or three times with him, and Frank get to hear of it, I suppose there would be a noble rampage: *then* he might speak out a little more.'

'Have you been dreaming, Madge?' said Nan, again staring at her sister. 'What has put such monstrous things into your head? Mr. Hanbury—at the Kenyons' — and you would dance with him!'

'Well, why not?' said Madge, with a frown; for this difficulty about the letter-writing had clearly operated on her temper and made her impatient. 'All the world isn't supposed to know about the Vice-Chancellor's warning. Why shouldn't he be invited by the Kenyons? And why should he know that I am going? And why, if we both happen to be there, shouldn't we dance together? Human beings are human beings, in spite of Vice-Chancellors. They can't lock up a man for dancing with you? At all events, they can't lock me up, even if Jack is there.'

'Madge, put these things out of your head. You won't go to the Kenyons', for Captain King would not like it——'

'I don't think he'd take the trouble to object,' Madge interjected.

'And Mr. Hanbury won't be there;

and there will be no dancing, and no quarrel. If you wish to write to Captain King about what will interest him, write about what interests yourself. That he is sure to be interested in——'

'Well, but that is exactly what I can't write to him about. I know what I am interested in well enough. Edith has just told me Mr. Roberts has been pressing her to fix a time for their marriage. She thinks the end of April; so that they could be back in London for the latter end of the season. Now I think that would do very well for us too—and it is always nice for two sisters to get married on the same day—only Frank has never asked me a word about it, and how am I to write to him about it? So you see, wise Mother Nan, I can't write to him about what interests me.'

Nan had started somewhat when she heard this proposal; it seemed strange to her.

'April?' she said. 'You've known Captain King a very short time, Madge. You were not thinking of getting married in April next?'

'Perhaps I'd better wait until I'm asked,' said Madge, with a laugh, as she turned to go away. 'Well, if you won't tell me what to write about, I must go and get this bothered letter done somehow. I do believe the best way will be to write about you; that will interest him anyway.'

Frank King remained away for a few weeks, and during this time the first symptoms appeared of the coming spring. The days began to lengthen, there were crocuses in the gardens, there were reports

of primroses and sweet violets in the woods
about Horsham ; in London Parliament
was sitting, and in Brighton well-known
faces were recognisable amongst the
promenaders on the Saturday afternoons.
Then Mr. Roberts, as Edith's accepted
suitor, received many invitations to the
house in Brunswick Terrace ; and in return
was most indefatigable in arranging riding-
parties, driving - parties, walking - parties,
with in each case a good hotel for luncheon
as his objective point. Madge joined in
these diversions with great good-will ; and
made them the excuse for the shortness
of the letters addressed to Kingscourt.
Nan went also ; she was glad to get into
the country on any pretence ; and she
seemed merry enough. When Mr. Roberts
drove along the King's Road with these
three comely damsels under his escort, he

was a proud man ; and he may have com-
forted himself with the question, that as
beer sometimes led to a baronetcy, why
shouldn't soda-water ?

Strangely enough, Nan had entirely
ceased making inquiries about sisterhoods
and institutions for the training of nurses.
She seemed quite reconciled to the situation of things as they were.   She did not
cease her long absences from the house ;
but every one knew that on these occasions
she was off on one of her solitary wanderings ; and she came home in the evening
apparently more contented than ever.   She
had even brought herself to speak of
Madge's married life, which at first she
would not do.

'You see,' she said to her sister on one
occasion, 'if you and Edith get married
on the same day, I must remain and take

care of mamma; she must not be left quite alone.'

'Oh, as for that,' said Madge, 'Mrs. Arthurs does better than the whole of us; and I'm not going to have you made a prisoner of. I'm going to have a room at Kingscourt called "Nan's room," and it shall have no other name as long as I am there. Then we shall have a proper house in London by and by; and of course you'll come up for the season, and see all the gaieties. I think we ought to have one of the red houses just by Prince's; that would be handy for everything; and you might come up, Nan, and help me to buy things for it. And you shall have a room there too, you shall; and you may decorate it and furnish it just as you like. I know quite well what you would like—the room small; the woodwork all bluey-white;

plenty of Venetian embroidery flung about; all the fire-place brass; some of those green Persian plates over the mantelpiece; about thirteen thousand Chinese fans arranged like fireworks on the walls; a fearful quantity of books and a low easy-chair; red candles; and in the middle of the whole thing a nasty, dirty, little beggar-girl to feed and pet——'

'I think, Madge,' her sister said, gravely, 'that you should not set your heart on a town-house at all.   Remember, old Mr. King is giving his son Kingscourt at a great sacrifice.   As I understand it, it will be a long time before the family estate is what it has been; and you would be very ungrateful if you were extrava-gant———'

'Oh, I don't see that,' said Madge. 'They are conferring no favour on me.

I don't see why I should economise. I
am marrying for fun, not for love.'

She blurted out this inadvertently—to
Nan's amazement and horror—but instantly retracted it, with the blood rush-
ing to her temples.

'Of course I don't mean that, Nan—
how could I have been so stupid! I don't
mean *that—exactly*. What I mean is that
it doesn't seem to me as if it was supposed
to be a very fearfully romantic match, and
all that kind of thing. It's a very good
arrangement; but it isn't I who ought to
be expected to make sacrifices——'

'But surely your husband's interests
will be yours!' exclaimed Nan.

'Oh yes, certainly,' her sister said,
somewhat indifferently. 'No doubt that's
true, in a way. Quite true, in a kind of
way. Still, there are limits; and I should

not like to be buried alive for ever in the country.'

Then she sighed.

' Poor Jack !' she said.

She went to the window.

' When I marry, I know at least one who will be sorry.   I can fancy him walking up and down there—looking at the house as he used to do ; and, oh ! so grateful if only you went to the window for a moment. He will see it in the papers, I suppose.'

She turned to her sister, and said, trium- phantly—

' Well, the Vice-Chancellor was done that time !'

' What time ?'

' Valentine's morning.   You can send flowers without any kind of writing to be traced.   Do you think I don't know who sent me the flowers ?'

'At all events, you should not be proud of it. You should be sorry. It is a very great pity——'

'Yes, that's what I think,' said Madge. 'How can I help pitying him? It wouldn't be natural not to pity him, Vice-Chancellor or no Vice-Chancellor. I hate that man.'

'I say it is a great pity that Mr. Hanbury does not accept his dismissal as inevitable; and as for you, Madge, you ought not even to think of him. Captain King sent you that beautiful card-case on Valentine's morning; that is what you should remember.'

'Captain King could send me a white elephant if he chose,' said Madge, spitefully. 'There's no danger to him in anything he does. It's different with poor Jack.'

'Madge,' said her sister, seriously, 'do

you know that you are talking as if you looked forward to this marriage with regret ?'

' Oh no, I don't—I'm not such a fool,' said Madge, plainly. ' I know it's stupid to think about Jack Hanbury; but still, one has got a little feeling.'

Then she laughed.

' I will tell you another secret, Nan. If he daren't write to me, he can send me things. He sent me a book—a novel— and I know he meant me to think the hero himself. For he was disappointed in love, too, and wrote beautifully about his sufferings, and at last the poor fellow blew his brains out.'

' Well, Mr. Hanbury couldn't do that, at all events—for reasons,' Nan said.

' Now that is a very bad joke,' said Madge, in a sudden outburst of temper;

'an old, stupid, bad joke, that has been made a hundred times. I'm ashamed of you, Nan. They say you have a great sense of humour; that's when you say things they can't understand; and they pretend to have a great sense of humour too. But where's the humour in that?'

'But Madge, dear,' said Nan, gently, 'I didn't mean to say anything against Mr. Hanbury——'

'In any case, there is one in this house who does not despise Mr. Hanbury for being poor,' said Madge, hotly. 'It isn't his fault that his papa and mamma haven't given him money and sent him out into the world to buy a wife!'

And therewith she quickly went to the door and opened it, and went out and shut it again with something very closely resembling a slam.

CHAPTER XXI.

DANGER AHEAD.

Nan waited the return of Frank King with the deepest anxiety. She would see nothing in these wild words of Madge's but an ebullition of temper. She could not bring herself to believe that her own sister—a girl with everything around her she could desire in the world—would deliberately enter upon one of those hateful marriages of convenience. It was true, Nan had to confess to herself, that Madge was not very impressionable. There was no great depth in her nature. Then she

was a trifle vain, and liked admiration;
and she was evidently pleased to have a
handsome and certainly eligible suitor.
But no—it was impossible that she had
really meant what she said. When Captain King came back, then the true state
of affairs would be seen. Madge was not
going to marry for money or position—or
even out of spite.

And when Frank King did come back,
matters looked very well at first. Madge
received him in a very nice, friendly fashion,
and was pleased by certain messages from
the old folks at Kingscourt. Nan's fears
began to fade away. Nothing more was
heard of Jack Hanbury. So far as Madge
was concerned everything seemed right.

But Nan, who was very anxious, and on
that account unusually sensitive, seemed
to detect something strange in Frank

King's manner. He had nothing of the
gay audacity of an accepted suitor. When
he paid Madge any little attention, it appeared almost an effort. He was preoccupied and thoughtful; sometimes, after regarding Madge in silence, he would apparently wake up to the consciousness that
he ought to be more attentive to her; but
there did not seem to be much joyousness
in their relationship. When these two
happened to be together—during the morning stroll down the Pier, or on the way
home from church, or seated at a concert
—they did not seem to have many things
to speak about. Frank King grew more
and more grave; and Nan saw it, and
wondered, and quite failed to guess at
the reason.

The fact was that he had now discovered
what a terrible mistake he had made. He

could blind himself no longer. Madge was not Nan; nor anything approaching to Nan; they were as different as day and night. Face to face with this discovery, he asked himself what he ought to do. Clearly, if he had made a mistake, it was his first duty that no one else should suffer by it. Because he was disappointed in not finding in Madge certain qualities and characteristics he had expected to find, he was not going to withdraw from an en-gagement he had voluntarily entered into. It was not Madge's fault. If the prospect of this marriage pleased her, he was bound to fulfil his promise. After all, Madge had her own qualities. Might they not wear as well through the rough work of the world, even if they had not for him the fascination he had hoped for? In any case, the disappointment should be his,

not hers. She should not suffer any slight.
And then he would make another desperate
resolve to be very affectionate and attentive
to her; resolves which usually ended in
his carrying to her some little present of
flowers, or something like that, having
presented which, he would turn and talk
to Nan.

'I say, Beresford,' he suddenly observed,
one night at dinner, ' I have an invitation
to go salmon-fishing in Ireland. Will you
come ?'

'Well, but—— ' Madge interposed,
with an injured air, as if she ought to have
been consulted first.

' I should like it tremendously!' said
Mr. Tom, with a rush.

'I am told the scenery in the neighbourhood is very fine,' continued Captain King;
'at all events we are sure to think so half

a dozen years hence. That is one of the grand points about one's memory; you forget all the trivial details and discomforts, and only remember the best.'

He quite naturally turned to Nan.

'I am sure, Miss Nan,' he said, 'you have quite a series of beautiful little pictures in your mind about that Splügen excursion. Don't you remember the drive along the Via Mala, in the shut-up carriage—the darkness outside—and the swish of the rain——'

'Well,' said Madge, somewhat spitefully, 'considering you were in a closed carriage and driving through darkness, I don't see much of a beautiful picture to remember!'

He did not seem to heed. It was Nan he was addressing; and there was a pleased light in her eyes. Reminiscences are to some people very delightful things.

'And you recollect the crowded saloon in the Splügen inn, and the snug little corner we got near the stove, and the little table. That's where you discovered the use of stupid people at dinner-parties——'

'What's that?' Mr. Tom demanded to know.

'It's a secret,' Captain King answered, with a laugh. 'And I think you were rather down-hearted next morning—until we began to get up through the clouds. That is a picture to remember at all events —a Christmas picture in summer time. Do you remember how green the pines looked above the snow? And how blue the sky was when the mist got driven over? And how business-like you looked in your ulster—buttoned up to the chin for resolute Alpine work. I fancy I can hear now the

very chirp of your boots on the wet snow
—it was very silent away up there.'

'I know,' said Nan, somewhat shamefacedly, 'that when I saw "*Ristoratore*"
stuck up on the house near the top, I
thought it was a place for restoring people
found in the snow, until I heard the driver
call out "*Du, hole Schnapps.*"'

'Wasn't that a wild whirl down the other
side!' he continued, delightedly. 'But
you should have come into the Customs-
house with me when I went to declare my
cigars. You see it wouldn't do for me,
who might one day get a coastguard ap-
pointment, to try on any smuggling. But
I did remonstrate. I said I had already
paid at Paris and at Basel; and that it
was hard to have to pay three import dues
on my cigars. Well, they were very civil.
They said they couldn't help it. "Why

not buy your cigars in the country where you smoke them ?" asked an old gentleman in spectacles. " Because, Monsieur," I answered him, with the usual cheek of the English, " I prefer to smoke cigars made of tobacco." But he was quite polite. After charging me eighteen francs, he bowed me out, and said " a rivederla ;" to which I responded " Oh, no, thank you ;" and then I found you and your sisters all laughing at me, as if I had been before a police-magistrate to be admonished.'

'You don't forget all the disagreeable details, then ?' said Nan, with a smile.

But the smile vanished from her face when he began to talk about Bellagio. He did so without any covert intention. It was always a joy to him to think or talk about the time that he and the three sisters spent together far away there in the south.

And it was only about the *Serenata* and the procession of illuminated boats that he was thinking at this moment.

'I suppose they will sooner or later have all our ships and steamers lit with the electric light; and everything will be ghastly white and ghastly black. But do you remember how soft and beautiful the masses of yellow stars were when the boats came along the lake in the darkness? It was indeed a lovely night. And I think we had the best of it—sitting there in the garden. I know I for one didn't miss the music a bit. And then it was still more lovely when the moon rose; and you could see the water, and the mountains on the other side, and even the houses by the shore. I remember there was a bush somewhere near us that scented all the air——'

Madge had been regarding her sister closely.

' It must have been a magical night,' she said quickly, ' for Nan's face has got quite white just thinking of it.'

He started. A quick glance at the girl beside him showed him that she was indeed pale ; her eyes cast down ; her hand trembling. Instantly he said, in a confused hurry,—

' You see, Miss Anne, there was some delay about the concert. One steamer did really come back to Bellagio. We had our serenade all the same—that is to say, any who were awake. You see, they did not intend to swindle you——'

' Oh, no ! oh, no !' said Nan ; and then, conscious that Madge was still regarding her, she added with a desperate effort at composure,—

'We heard some pretty music on the water at Venice. Edith picked up some of the airs. She will play them to you after dinner.'

That same night, as usual, Madge came into Nan's room, just before going off.

'Nan,' she said, looking straight at her, 'what was it upset you about Frank's reminding you of Bellagio?'

'Bellagio?' repeated Nan, with an effort to appear unconscious, but with her eyes turned away.

'Yes; you know very well.'

'I know that I was thinking of something quite different from anything that Captain King was saying,' Nan said, at length. 'And—and it is of no consequence to you, Madge, believe me.'

Madge regarded her suspiciously for a second, and then said, with an air of triumph,

'At all events, he isn't going to Ireland.'

'Oh, indeed,' Nan answered, gently. 'Well I'm glad; I suppose you prefer his not going?'

'It nearly came to a quarrel, I know,' said Madge, frankly. 'I thought it just a bit too cool. At all events, he ought to pretend to care a little for me.'

'Oh, Madge, how can you say such things? Care for you—and he has asked you to be his wife! Could he care for you more than that?'

'He has never even thanked me for not going to the Kenyons' ball,' said Madge, who appeared to imagine that Nan was responsible for everything Captain King did or did not do.

'Surely he would take it for granted you would not go!' remonstrated the elder sister.

'But he takes everything for granted. And he scarcely ever thinks it worth while to speak to me. And I know it will be a regular bore when we go to Kingscourt, with the old people still there, and me not mistress at all; and what am I to do?'

She poured out this string of wild complaints rapidly and angrily.

'Good-night, Madge,' said Nan; 'I am rather tired to-night.'

'Good-night. But I can tell you if he hadn't given up Ireland, there would have been a row.'

It was altogether a strange condition of affairs; and next day it was apparently made worse. There had been a stiffish gale blowing all night from the south; and in the morning, though the sky was cloudless, there was a heavy sea running, so that from the windows they saw white

masses of foam springing into the air—
hurled back by the sea-wall at the end of
Medina Terrace. When Captain King
came along Mr. Tom at once proposed
they should all of them take a stroll as far
as the Terrace; for now the tide was full
up and the foam was springing into the
blue sky to a most unusual height. And,
indeed, when they arrived they found a
pretty big crowd collected; a good many
of whom had obviously been caught unawares by the shifting and swirling masses
of spray. It was a curious sight. First
the great wave came rolling on with but
little beyond an ominous hissing noise;
then there was a heavy shock that made
the earth tremble, and at the same
moment a roar as of thunder; then into
the clear sky rose a huge wall of gray,
illuminated by the sunlight, and showing

clearly and blackly the big stones and
smaller shingle that had been caught and
whirled up in the seething mass. Occasionally a plank of drift timber was similarly whirled up—some thirty or forty feet ;
disappearing altogether again as it fell
crashing into the roar of the retreating
wave. It was a spectacle, moreover, that
changed every few seconds, as the heavy
volumes of the sea hit the breakwater at
different angles. The air was thick with
the salt spray ; and hot with the sunlight
—even on this March morning.

Then it became time for Mr. Tom and
Captain Frank to go and witness a chal-
lenge game of rackets that had been much
talked of ; and the girls walked back with
them as far as Brunswick Terrace, Madge
being with Frank King.

'Why is it one never sees Mr. Jacomb
now ?' he asked of his companion.

'I saw him only the other day,' she said evasively.

'But he does not come to the house, does he?'

'N—no,' said Madge.

'Has he left Brighton?'

'Oh no,' answered Madge, and she drew his attention to a brig that was making up Channel under very scant sail indeed.

'I daresay he has a good deal of work to do,' said Frank King absently. 'When are they going to be married?'

Madge saw that the revelation could be put off no longer.

'Oh, but they are not going to be married. Nan isn't going to be married at all.'

He stared at her, as if he had scarcely heard her aright; and then he said slowly—

'Nan isn't going to be married? Why have you never told me before?'

'Oh, it is a private family matter,' said Madge, petulantly. 'It is not to be talked about. Besides, how could I know it would interest you?'

He remained perfectly silent and thoughtful. They walked along. Madge began to think she had been too ungracious.

'I suppose she tried to bring herself to it for a time,' she said, more gently. 'She has wonderful ideas, Nan has; and I suppose she thought she could do a deal of good as a clergyman's wife. For my part, I don't see what she could do more than she does at present. It's just what she's fit for. Poor people don't resent her going into their houses as they would if it was you or I. She manages it somehow. That's how she gets to know all about out-of-the-way sort of things; she's practical;

and people think it strange that a young
lady like her should know the ways and
habits of common people ; and that's why
she interests them when she talks. There's
nothing wonderful in it. Anybody can
find out what the profit is on selling
oranges, if you like to go and talk to a
hideous old wretch who is smelling of gin.
But I don't say anything against Nan.
It's her way. It's what she was intended
for by Providence, I do believe. But she
was sold that time she wanted to get up
a little committee to send a constant sup-
ply of books and magazines to the lighthouses—circulating, you know. She wrote
to Sir George about it ; and found the
Admiralty did that already.'

There was a strange, hopeless, tired
look on this man's face. He did not
seem to hear her. He appeared to know

nothing of what was going on around him.

When they reached the door of the house, he said,—

' Good-bye !'

' Good-bye ?' she repeated, inquiringly. ' I thought we were all going to see the Exhibition of Paintings this afternoon.'

' I think I must go up to London for a few days,' he said, with some hesitation. ' There—is some business——— '

She said no more ; but turned and went indoors without a word. He bade good-bye to Edith and to Nan—not looking into Nan's face at all. Then he left with the brother, and Mr. Tom was silent, for his friend King seemed much disturbed about something, and he did not wish to worry him.

As for Madge, she chose to work her-

self into a pretty passion, though she said
nothing.   That she should have been
boasting of her triumph in inducing, or
forcing, him to give up that visit to Ireland
only to find him going off to London without warning or explanation, was altogether
insufferable.   She was gloomy and morose
all the afternoon ; would not go to see the
pictures ; refused to come in and speak to
certain callers ; and at dinner made a little
show of sarcasm that did not hurt anybody
very much.

The evening brought her a letter.   Thus
it ran :—

'Dear Madge—I thought you looked
angry when you went indoors this morning.   Don't quarrel about such a trifle as
my going to London.   I shall be back in
two or three days ; and hope to bring
with me the big photograph of Kings-

court, if they have got any copies printed yet.   Your F<small>RANK</small>.'

'From whom is your letter, Madge?' Lady Beresford said, incidentally.

'From Frank, mamma,' said the young lady, as she quietly and determinedly walked across the room and—thrust it into the fire!

That same night Miss Madge also wrote a note; but the odd thing was that the writing of both note and address was in a disguised hand. And when, some little time thereafter, the others were in the billiard-room, it was Madge herself who slipped out from the house and went and dropped that missive into the nearest pillar letter-box.

CHAPTER XXII.

A CATASTROPHE.

HOWEVER, Madge's ill-temper was never of long duration; and at this particular time, instead of sinking farther into sulks over the absence of her lover, she grew day by day more joyous and generous and affectionate. The change was most marked; and Nan, who was her sister's chief confidant, could not make it out at all. Her gaiety became almost hysterical; and her kindness to everybody in the house ran to extravagance. She bought trinkets for the servants. She presented

Mr. Tom with a boot-jack mounted in silver; and he was pleased to say that it was the first sensible present he had ever known a girl make. But it was towards Nan that she was most particularly affectionate and caressing.

'You know I'm not clever, Nan,' she said, in a burst of confidence, 'and I haven't got clockworks in my brain, and I daresay I'm not interesting—*to every-body*. But I know girls who are stupider than I am who are made plenty of. And of course, if you don't have any romance when you're young, when are you likely to get it after?'

'But I don't know what you mean, Madge!' Nan exclaimed.

Nor did Madge explain at the moment. She continued—

'I believe it was you, Nan, who told me

of the young lady who remarked, " What's the use of temptation if you don't yield to it ?" '

'That was only a joke,' said Nan, with her demure smile.

' Oh, I think there's sense in it,' said the practical Madge. ' It doesn't do to be too wise when you're young.'

' It so seldom happens, Madge !' said her sister.

' There you are again, old Mother Hubbard, with your preaching! But I'm not going to quarrel with you this time. I want your advice. I want you to tell me what little thing I should buy for Frank, just to be friends all round, don't you know ?'

' Friends ? Yes, I hope so!' said Nan, with a grave smile. ' But how can I tell you, Madge ? I don't know, as you ought to know, what Captain King has in the way of cigar-cases or such things——'

'But call him Frank, Nan! Do, to please me. And I know he would like it.'

'Some time I may,' said Nan evasively. 'Afterwards, perhaps.'

'When you come to Kingscourt,' said Madge, with a curious kind of laugh.

Nan was silent, and turned away ; she never seemed to wish to speak of Kingscourt or her going there.

Frank King's stay in London was prolonged for some reason or other ; at length he announced his intention of returning to Brighton on a particular Thursday. On the Tuesday night Nan and Madge arranged that they would get fresh flowers the next day for the decoration of the rooms.

'And this is what I will do for you, Madge, as it is a special occasion,' remarked Miss Anne, with grave patronage. 'If you will get up early to-morrow, I will take you to a place, not more than four miles off, where you will find any quantity of hart's-tongue fern. It is a deep ditch, I suppose a quarter of a mile long, and the banks are covered. Of course I don't want any one to know, for it is so near Brighton it would be harried for the shops; but I will show you the place, as you will soon be going away now ; and we can take a basket.'

'But how did you find it out, Nan ?'

'Some one showed it to me.'

'The singing-woman, I suppose ?'

'Yes. Think of that. I believe she could get twopence a root ; and she might fill a cart there. But she won't touch one.'

'No,' said Edith, with a superior smile. 'She leaves that for young ladies who could very well afford to go to a florist's.'

'What I shall take won't hurt,' said Nan, meekly.

So, next morning, Nan got up about eight; dressed, and was ready to start. That is to say, she never arranged her programme for the day with the slightest respect to meals. So long as she could get an apple and a piece of bread to put in her pocket she felt provided against everything. However, she thought she would go along to Madge's room, and see if that young lady had ideas about breakfast.

Madge's room was empty; and Nan thought it strange she should have gone downstairs without knocking at her door in passing. But when Nan also went below she found that Madge had left the house before any one was up. She could not understand it at all.

Mr. Tom came down.

'Oh,' said he, indifferently, 'she wants to be mighty clever and find out those ferns for herself.'

'But I did not tell her where they were. I only said they were on the road to —— ' said Nan, naming the place : the writer has reasons of his own for not being more explicit.

'All the cleverer if she can find out. The cheek of the young party is pyramidal,' said Mr. Tom, as he rang for breakfast.

But at lunch, also, Madge had not turned up.

'It is very extraordinary,' said Lady Beresford, though she was too languid to be deeply concerned.

'Oh no, it isn't, mother,' said Mr. Tom. 'It's all Nan's fault. Nan has infected her. The Baby, you'll see, has taken to tramping about the country with gypsies; and prowling about farmers' kitchens; and catching leverets, and stuff. We lives on the simple fruits of the earth, my dears; we eats of the root, and we drinks of the spring; but that doesn't prevent us having a whacking appetite somewhere about seven forty-five. Edith, my love, pass me the cayenne-pepper.'

'Boys shouldn't use cayenne-pepper,' said Nan.

'And babies should speak only when they're spoken to,' he observed. 'Mother, dear, I have arrived at the opinion that Madge has run away with young Hanbury. I am certain of it. The young gentleman is fool enough for anything——'

'You always were spiteful against Mr. Hanbury,' said Edith, 'because his feet are smaller than yours.'

'My love,' retorted Mr. Tom, with imperturbable good-nature, 'his feet may be small. It is in his stupidity that he is really great. Jack Hanbury can only be described in the words of the American poet : he is a commodious ass.'

Now this conjecture of Mr. Tom's about the cause of Madge's disappearance was only a piece of gay facetiousness. It never did really occur to him that any one —that any creature with a head capable of being broken—would have the wild audacity to run away with one of his sisters, while he, Mr. Tom Beresford, was to the fore. But that afternoon post brought Nan a letter. She was amazed to see by the handwriting that it was from Madge ;

she was still more alarmed when she read these words, scrawled with a trembling hand, and in pencil:

'Dearest, dearest Nan, don't be angry. By the time you get this Jack and I will be married. It is all for the best, dear Nan; and you will pacify them; and it is no use following us; for we shall be in France until it is all smoothed down. Not a single bridesmaid—we daren't—but what wouldn't I do for Jack's sake? It is time I did something to make up for all he has suffered—he was looking so ill—in another month he would have *died.* He worships me. You never saw anything like it. Jack has just come back; so good-bye; from your loving, loving sister, MARGARET HANBURY.—Do you know who that is, Nan?'

Nan, not a little frightened, took the

letter to her brother, and gave it him without a word.   But Mr. Tom's rage was at once prompt and voluble.   That she should have disgraced the family—for, of course, the whole thing would be in the papers!   That she should have cheated and jilted his most particular friend!   But as for this fellow Hanbury——

' I said it all along.   I told you what would come of it!   I knew that fellow was haunting her like a shadow.   Well, we'll see how a shadow likes being locked up on bread and water.   Oh, it's no use your protesting, Nan; I will let the law take its course.   We'll see how he likes that.   " Stone walls do not a prison make" —that's what love-sick fellows say ; don't they?   Wait a bit.   Mr. Jack Hanbury will find that stone walls make a very good imitation of a prison, at all events——'

'But, Tom—dear Tom,' Nan pleaded, 'it is no use making matters worse. Let us try to make them better. If Madge is married, it can't be helped now. We must make the best of it——'

He paid no attention to her; he was still staring at the ill-written letter.

'That's all gammon about their going to France. He hasn't money for travelling. She spent all hers in nick-nacks—to propitiate people, the sneak! They're in London.'

He looked at his watch.

'I can just catch the 5.45 express. Nan, you go and tell the others; they needn't squawk about it all over Brighton.'

'What are you going to do, Tom?' said his sister, breathlessly.

'Find out where they are first. Then Colonel Fitzgerald and Mr. Mason must take it up. Then Mr. Jack Hanbury will suddenly find himself inside Millbank prison.'

She caught him by the hand.

'Tom, is it wise?' she pleaded again. They are married. What is the use of revenge? You don't want to make your own sister miserable?——'

'She has brought it on herself,' he said, roughly.

'Then that is what I am to think of you,' she said, regarding him, 'that some day I may hear you talk in that way about me?'

He never could resist the appeal of Nan's clear, faithful eyes.

'You wouldn't be such a fool,' he said. 'And they won't touch Madge. It's only that fellow they'll go for—the mean hound, to marry a girl for her money.'

'How do you know it was for her money, Tom?' Nan pleaded. 'I am certain they were fond of each other——'

'I don't want to miss my train,' said he. 'You go and tell the maternal I'm off to London. I suppose you don't know the address of Hanbury's father?'

'No, I don't.'

'Well, I'm off. Ta, ta!'

So the irate Mr. Tom departed. But in the comparative silence of the Pullman car the fury of his rage began to abate; and it dawned upon him that, after all, Nan's counsel might have something in it. No doubt these two young fools—as he mentally termed them—were married by this time. He still clung to the idea that Jack Hanbury deserved punishment—a horse-whipping or something of the kind; but Madge was Madge. She was silly;

and she had 'got into a hole;' still, she was Madge. She might be let off with a serious lecture on her folly and on her disregard of what she owed to the other members of the family. Only, the first thing was to find out their whereabouts.

On arriving in London he drove to his club, and after some little searching discovered that Mr. Gregory Hanbury's address was Adelphi Terrace, whither he at once repaired. Mr. Hanbury was at dinner. He sent up his card nevertheless, and asked to be allowed to see Mr. Hanbury on particular business. The answer was a request that he would step upstairs into the dining-room.

He found that occupied by two gentlemen who were dining together at the upper end of a large table. One came forward to meet him. He took it for granted this was Mr. Hanbury—a slight, short man, with black hair and eyes, and a very stiff white cravat.

'Mr. Beresford,' said he, 'I can guess what has brought you here. Let me introduce you to my brother—Major Hanbury. It is an unfortunate business.'

The other gentleman—also slight and short, but with a sun-browned, dried-up face, and big gray moustache—bowed and resumed his seat.

'You know, then, that your son has run away with my sister,' said Mr. Tom, somewhat hotly—though he had determined to keep his temper. 'Perhaps you know also where they are?'

'No farther,' said the black-haired gentleman, with perfect calmness, 'than that I believe them to be in London. It is only about a couple of hours since I

heard of the whole affair. I immediately
sent for my brother. It is a most distressing business altogether. Of course you
are chiefly concerned for your sister; but
my son is in a far more serious position.'

'Yes, I should think so!' exclaimed
Mr. Tom. 'I should think he was! But
you don't know where they are?'

'No; I only know they are in London.
I received a letter from my son this afternoon, asking me to intercede for him with
the Court of Chancery; and it is from this
letter that I learn how serious his position
is—more serious than he seems to imagine.
He appears to think that now the marriage has taken place, the Vice-Chancellor
will condone everything——'

'He won't: I will take good care that
he shan't!' Mr. Tom said.

'My dear sir, I am sorry to say that my

son is in a very awkward situation, even although no personal vindictiveness be shown towards him. Your sister is not of age, I believe ?'

'Of course not. She's just turned eighteen.'

'Ah. Then, you see, Jack had to declare that she was of age. And he appears to have stated that he had resided three weeks in the parish, whereas he only came up from Brighton yesterday morning. And, again, marrying in the direct teeth of an order of the Court—I am afraid, sir, that he is in a bad enough predicament without any personal vengeance being shown him.'

This seemed to strike Mr. Tom.

'I don't hit a man when he's down. I will let the law take its course. I shan't interfere.'

' Don't you think, sir,' said this man
with the calm black eyes and the quiet
manner, ' that it might be wiser, in the
interests of your sister, if you were to help
us to arrange some amicable settlement
which we could put before the Court ?   I
believe the guardians of the young lady
were very much misinformed about my
son's character and his intentions with
regard to her.   I am certain that it was
not her fortune that attracted him, or that
could have led him into the perilous position he now occupies.   Now, if we could
go before the Vice-Chancellor, and say,
" The marriage is not so unsuitable, after
all.   The young man comes of a highly
respectable family.   His relations (that is,
my brother and myself, sir,) are willing to
place a substantial sum at his disposal for
investment in a sound business—indeed,

there is a brewery at Southampton that
my brother has just been speaking
of——'

'A brewery!' exclaimed Mr. Tom ; but
he instantly recollected that beer was as
good as soda-water from a social point of
view.

'And if we could say to the Vice-Chancellor that the friends of the young lady
were willing to condone his offence —
always providing, of course, and naturally,
that your sister's fortune should be strictly
settled upon herself—then, perhaps, he
might be let off with a humble apology to
the Court ; and the young people be left
to their own happiness. My dear sir, we
lawyers see so much of the inevitable hardship of human life that when a chance
occurs of friendly compromise——'

'That's all very well,' blurted out Mr.

Tom. 'But I call it very mean and shabby of him to inveigle my sister away like that. She was engaged to be married to an old friend of mine ; a much better fellow, I'll be bound ! I call it very shabby.'

' My dear sir,' said the lawyer, placidly, ' I do not seek for a moment to excuse my son's conduct, except to remind you that at a certain period of life romance counts for something. I believe many young ladies are like the young lady in the play—I really forget what her name was—who was disappointed to find that she was not to be run away with. However, that is a different matter. I put it to you whether it would not be better for every one concerned if we were to try to arrive at an amicable arrangement, and give the young people a fair start in life.'

'Of course I can't answer for all our side,' said Mr. Tom, promptly. 'You'd better come with me to-morrow, and we'll talk it over with Colonel Fitzgerald and Mr. Mason. I don't bear malice. I think what you say is fair and right—if the settlement is strict. And if it came to be a question of interceding, there's an old friend of ours, Sir George Stratherne, who, I know, knows the Vice-Chancellor very intimately——'

'My dear sir!' the lawyer protested, with either real or affected horror, ' do not breathe such a thing!—do not think of such a thing. The duty of the Vice-Chancellor to his wards is of the extremest kind ; his decisions are beyond suspicion ; what we have got to say we must say in open court.'

' But if they were to lock your son up in

prison,' said Mr. Tom, with a gentle smile, 'that couldn't prevent Sir George taking my sister to call on the Vice-Chancellor some afternoon at his own house. And Madge is rather pretty. And she might cry.'

'Will you take a glass of wine, Mr. Beresford ?' said the lawyer, effusively; for he saw that he had quite won over Mr. Tom to his side.

' No, thank you,' said the latter, rising ; ' I must apologise for interrupting your dinner. I'll look up Colonel Fitzgerald and Mason to-morrow morning ; and bring them along here most likely ; that will be the simplest way. I suppose you are likely to know sooner than any one where these two fugitives have got to ?'

' I think so. I have sent an advertisement to the morning papers. I shall certainly counsel my son to surrender at once and throw himself on the mercy of the Court. My dear sir, I am exceedingly obliged to you for your kindness, your very great kindness, in calling.'

'Oh, don't mention it,' said Mr. Tom, going to the door. And then he added, ruefully, 'Now I've got to go and hunt up my friend; and tell him that my own sister has jilted him. You've no idea what a treat that will be!'

END OF VOL. II.

Printed by R. & R. CLARK, *Edinburgh.*